D1708388

WHO KNEW?

Lessons from My First Forty Years

Christine R. Andola

ARCHWAY
PUBLISHING

Archway Publishing books may be ordered
through booksellers or by contacting:

Archway Publishing
1663 Liberty Drive
Bloomington, IN 47403
www.archwaypublishing.com
1 (888) 242-5904

ISBN: 978-1-4808-3815-4 (sc)
ISBN: 978-1-4808-3816-1 (e)

Library of Congress Control Number: 2016916416

Print information available on the last page.

Archway Publishing rev. date: 2/21/2017

CONTENTS

INTRODUCTION

When I step up to the podium to accept the award for being the best me I can be...wearing the most elegant magenta gown you've ever seen, form fitted to my ten-pounds-lighter-than-reality body with my hair swept up in an intricate pile on top of my head, my earlobes dripping with real diamonds, and my toes jammed into a pair of gorgeous shoes shaped like pizza slices with tall skinny heels...I will thank the universe.

I want to thank the universe for aligning its cosmic forces to create some of the pivotal moments in my life. I could not have become the best me possible without that moment when I lost my job in the middle of a recession, and it rained for a week straight. Or how about the time I drove that rented camper into the gas station not designed to accommodate the turning radius of a 34 foot vehicle. Happily, that moment took place just before I picked up Grandma and Grandpa for our four-day road trip.

The Universe has allowed me, on countless occasions, the opportunity to learn, grow and test my abilities, if not my stamina. From showing me who my boyfriend really loved by a chance encounter, to taking my mother away just when we started to agree on things, to giving me chicken pox the second time, the Universe has been my great teacher. Coordinating that bout of the flu with the day my ex-husband and I separated, and I had to pack and move all alone for the first time, taught me about the strength of the human spirit in its determination to get out of a bad marriage.

The Universe constantly creates environments for me to exhibit my best stuff. Unfortunately, at some moments even my best stuff would be best kept secret — like that time I emerged from the ladies room in the middle of a party with my skirt caught up in my pantyhose. And let's not forget the highly descriptive, well-written, extremely personal email that was replicated on all of the computers in the school. Had the Universe not carefully orchestrated a number of coinciding factors there, I might never have learned that the "e" in email stands for "everybody."

I would not be here today, at the pinnacle of my career as myself, if it were not for the astute nature of nature to plunge me head first into the bottom of the pool after diving into the shallow end. Or to subject me to such a severe sunburn after pulling an all-nighter on the beach that my forehead swelled creating a Mongoloid profile. (Remember how people gasped when I walked down the street the next day?)

I want to thank the Universe for putting me here in this exact spot at this exact time. Without your great wisdom and convergence of forces, Universe, I would not be on my way to being the best me I can be.

And isn't that the big goal in life, to be the best me I can be? Or is it to avoid pain and turmoil, I always forget. Through some combination of striving and surviving, I managed to get through my first forty years. I had no idea this is what forty would look like, or feel like. In fact, this was not the image I had of my forty-year-old self twenty years ago.

But here I am on the verge of self-fulfillment (how big is a verge, anyway?) with nothing but the wisdom of forty years to show for my efforts. At some existential moment on the eve of my fortieth birthday, I realized it was all a waste unless I share my knowledge so that others get a chance to avoid some of my mis-steps and move right on to the hard stuff.

It's still not clear to me, or anyone who knows me really well, whether this book was born out of an altruistic sense of sharing or my instinct to instruct. Either way, the lessons contained within are yours to heed at will or dismiss with a silent eye-roll. You might be educated, entertained, enlightened, or amused by my stories. I hope it will be a little of each.

CHAPTER ONE

"...*family had definitely failed me. I was the innocent and naïve victim in all of this.*"

Where's the Function in Family?

It seems like a simple concept. Everyone has a family. The first thing you know about the world outside your skin is your family. You grow up with these people around you; they are your whole world at first. Then, you move beyond the boundaries of the family out into the wider world. You discover differences between yourself and others, many of which have to do with your family of origin.

You meet people who still go home for Sunday dinner, and those who haven't been home in years. You learn that while some value their shared name, others try to hide it. Some put family before all else and others only say they do. Families sometimes appear loving in public but fight in private, and some fight anywhere.

And by the time you're forty, you are so mixed up you don't know what family is all about, if you want a family, if there's a way to give yours up and join a different one, or if there is enough time left in your life for all the therapy that will be required to straighten out this mess.

I am happy to report on the eve of my fortieth birthday, that I am over my upbringing and have forgiven my parents for all the evil I once perceived they practiced on me. But it has been a colorful journey to this point. I have gone from never wanting to be like my mother to becoming much like her and happy about it. That doesn't happen over night.

Because I don't have kids of my own, I have been spared those instances in life when you hear your parent's voice emanating from your own lips. For better or worse, however, my mother's voice will live in my head always. And even when I don't share her insights with anyone, I still have to wrestle with them myself.

Parents Are Smarter Than You Think

My mother wanted to raise smart, independent girls. She didn't go in for make-up and curling irons, designer jeans or fashion magazines. But for some reason, from the time I was a little girl, I fancied myself a princess. I can remember blaming my mother when I wasn't popular in middle school. After all, she wouldn't allow me to have a curling iron or get my hair permed like all the other girls. How was I supposed to compete?

It seems as though my mother and I came at life from two different corners of the universe. Not really understanding much of my high school biology, I don't know how this is genetically possible. But now that I have gained the wisdom of forty years, I can say Mom was right about many things.

Yet, as I approached twenty I knew nothing of this insight and tortured the poor woman every time I opened my mouth. She tried to talk to me about declaring a major in college and having a career path, a reasonable conversation for a professional to have with her daughter. But I turned it into a life-lesson for Mom.

She eventually pushed the conversation to the point of mentioning that she and my father weren't going to feed and clothe me for the rest of my life and that I would have to assume that responsibility at some point. That's when I gently explained to her that I had no trouble getting a dinner date. I was not concerned because there would always be someone out there to feed me. Mom maintained her composure as I pranced out of the room, but I know now that she was rightfully horrified with my attitude.

Just a few years after her death, at the end of a failed marriage, I realized what Mom was trying to tell me. I woke up one day with a mortgage of my own and a job I hated. I realized there was no back-up plan. I would have to keep that horrible job in order to keep a roof over my head. Funny how life teaches the lessons parents can't.

I managed to finish college in four years because my parents had the logic and forethought I lacked. Each semester I came home and swore I was not going back. I hated college, couldn't understand what I was doing there, didn't see the value of it. They must have come to expect this confrontation because they developed a stock response. They would ask me what else I would do, recognizing that if I were not in college I would have to have a job and a place to live and all of that. I never came up with an alternate plan, so they packed me back off to college the following semester. In so many ways, I owe my college education, and any professional successes I've had as a result, to my parents. I couldn't see that when I was twenty, but I see it very clearly twenty years later.

The Blaming Years

I took that college degree I didn't want off into the world with high expectations, and so began the blaming years, which stretched well into my thirties. I'm not sure if the concept occurred to me on my own, or if the idea was planted by some well-meaning therapist. But I spent several of my first forty years blaming my parents — for everything!

The blaming years went well beyond that illusive genetic connection (why did I have to get my father's big nose). Actually, it was the physical traits I couldn't complain about. I am descendent from two generations of overweight people, yet I inherited shapely legs from both sides of the family (no tree-trunk legs here). And I got my maternal grandmother's thick hair and my father's long fingers while avoiding short stature on both sides of the family and the Northern Italian coarse hair.

No, the blaming was about everything I was not and everything that went "wrong" in my life. I spread the blame equally between my parents, Mom for dying and leaving me with her husband and children to deal with and Dad for not parenting me in her absence. I even threw some blame at society in general for leading me to believe that marriage would be easy.

I did everything that was expected of me — the big white dress, the traditional wedding, the handsome groom, the first family Christmas in our new house — but nobody bothered to tell me that just looking the part wouldn't be enough. It worked in all the movies but not in my life.

Once those rose-colored glasses were off and I could see that my family wasn't the perfect family-next-door, I set out to find out, "why me?" Suddenly I could see every flaw my parents had, every mistake they made. It was their fault. How could two professional educators do such a poor job of raising a child? And if they didn't know any better, what chance did everyone else's kids have of turning out to be normal, happy functioning members of society?

Oh, family had definitely failed me. I was the innocent and naïve victim in all of this. I did what they told me. I believed what they said. I followed our house rules, practiced our family traditions, sat still and quiet. I wore sneakers only for gym class, kept my shoes on at the dance. I made my bed every morning and helped clean the dishes after dinner. I watched out for my sisters, walked the dog when it was my turn, cut the grass when asked to. I went to college (though I had no idea what I was doing there) and came home with a degree.

So why couldn't I have a happy marriage, a full-filling career, a normal family? Why was I still afraid of the dark? Why didn't my in-laws like me? Why did I hate being a teacher? Why did I spontaneously burst into tears sometimes in public? Why didn't my family act like the ones on TV? Why did I feel so separate from everyone?

All of those questions have rather long intricate answers, none of which are really germane to this particular discussion — lucky for you! After spending several years blaming my parents for all of the evils in my life, shortly before approaching the end of my first forty years, I had an epiphany. It wasn't their fault!

My parents were good people who loved me very much. They did their best to raise me to be an intelligent, independent, conscientious woman, and for the most part it worked. My parents gave me the love and support and the material comforts they believed would benefit me in the long run. After nearly forty years on this planet, it was time for me to take over.

It is my responsibility to nurture myself as an adult. No more crying over "should've" and "could've". I have the ability to make my life whatever I want it to be. Of course, it is not as easy as it sounds, but that is the rightful order of things. Adults take responsibility and create their own happiness, set goals, make changes, re-evaluate and move on. My mother once told me that it was not important to marry a successful man because working toward success together was really what made life fun. She knew that life was in the striving, not the arriving. (And here I had spent the better part of forty years choosing an outfit for my arrival.)

While I spent most of my thirties blaming my parents for everything that was wrong with my life, they should have been in an institution recovering from my childhood. I don't know if there is a 12-step program for getting over the horrors of raising children, but there should be. My first forty years have taught me that parents are a blessing. We should treasure them, despite all their flaws and miss-steps, for their continued good intentions and unending love no matter how it is expressed.

Here are the basics:

- Parents are not perfect but none of us is.

- Parenting requires strength, patience, courage and a whole list of other qualities no one believes they actually possess.

- Your parents' way of doing something may not be the only way, but it is probably better than your way.

- Parents look at the world through the wisdom of experience which is much more accurate than the wisdom of adolescence.

Dysfunction Through The Generations

What I've noticed over these thirty-some years is that my perspective on family has come full circle. I began thinking all families were like mine. Then I learned about families that were different, and I thought mine was better. Then I saw that my family wasn't as great as I originally understood. Finally, I've come to the conclusion that all families are alike in their dysfunction. Maybe there is just something comforting about believing that everyone shares your pain.

Did you ever notice that everyone grew up in the same dysfunctional family? Tell a funny story about some grossly inappropriate event that took place between your family members and everyone listening is nodding his head and wearing a knowing smile.

When I was very young, my mother's parents and my father's parents tolerated each other enough to attend the same family functions. By the time I was a teenager, this was no longer the case. I can remember being a small child, maybe just three or four years old. I don't remember the occasion, but both of my grandfathers were in the living room with me. Someone set me down on the floor in the middle of the room and told me to go to the grandfather I liked the best. Despite my youth, I realized the awkwardness of the situation and just sat right down, refusing to move. As I grew up, I was occasionally put in similarly awkward situations between my two sets of grandparents.

It doesn't matter what neighborhood you grew up in, what religion you practiced, what country your grandparents came from, everyone has had the same experiences with family. All families have the "crazy one." Regardless of what they call that particular aunt, uncle, cousin, or grandfather, every family has the outcast member who acts, and probably thinks, differently from the rest of the family. After holiday gatherings, the phone lines are all abuzz with tales of what he or she did this time, and the posthumous reminiscence, snickering and giggling will go on forever.

My mother's mother had three sisters whom I got to know a little when I was growing up. From what I could tell, my grandmother was the ringleader, the second-born, and the bossy one. She has outlived them all, and in her early nineties and nearly blind she is bossy to this day. But the best stories were always about her sister Vera. Eyes rolled when Aunt Vera left the room. Everything Vera reported to the group was considered off the wall. It was often stated, though not to her face of course, that Vera was in her own world.

Aunt Vera vacationed with us once. The whole family was in Florida visiting my grandparents at the same time. In typical Florida fashion, we went out to dinner at 4:30 to beat the crowd, much to my father's chagrin. We sat fourteen strong around a huge table dead center in the restaurant. When the bill came, Aunt Vera made a scene insisting that she pay for her own meal. In the middle of one of those very uncomfortable dinner check scenes, Aunt Vera, who had more money than all the others combined, leaned over to my grandfather to borrow some cash to make good on her promise to pay for her own dinner.

Since I was still a child, many of the other things Aunt Vera was criticized for actually made some sense to me. I had a hard time understanding why Vera was always singled out as the crazy one. My grandmother probably had her reasons for discounting Vera's input all the time, reasons I'm sure I could never know or understand. That is another thing I've learned about family in forty years — a lot went on before I got here.

The relationships of the previous generations were not only established long before my birth, but they were developed in a time and place I have no real knowledge of. Some of the struggles of my grandparents and their siblings were over issues I have never faced — poverty, disease, and war. I have no way of truly understanding what it was like for them growing up and some elements of those relationships cannot be changed now.

You see, a lot of family dysfunction was created before I was born. Not that that removes my culpability, it just makes it harder to get to the bottom of things. Some days it almost seems easier to continue the flawed status quo than to try to sort it out. And, of course, genetics help push the family down those same paths.

I am the first born child in my family, a type A personality, a leader, and sometimes described as a real bitch. I have spent part of my forty years on this planet learning, understanding and accepting these facts, but not without a lot of questions and struggles. My father began pointing out my "flaws" in my early twenties by calling me Elvira - his mother's name. He once explained to the man I intended to marry that there are three very bossy women in our family - Elvira, Rose and Christine. I was simply continuing the bloodline from my father's mother through her favorite niece.

I had never looked at it that way, but I had always seen the similarities between Grandma Elvira and Cousin Rose. Grandma was an organizer. On the farm, she worked in the packinghouse during busy seasons. As the story goes, a handful of people would be frantically packing tomatoes when Grandma would yell, "Stop!" She would rearrange the assembly line, ordering people to move their chairs, change position, and work in a different direction. Then, she would re-start the work with the more efficient flow. Grandma was never afraid to speak her mind, as any waiter who ever brought her a substandard meal could attest. (When one waiter asked how her meal was, she responded, "They should take this off the menu.")

Cousin Rose had the same outspoken manner as Grandma. No one who knew them ever missed this connection. In some ways,

Rose seemed like the next generation of Grandma. Watching the two of them have a conversation was always interesting because they didn't spare each other the sharp barbs, either. It was like witnessing what each would say if she were confronted with her own attitude. They loved each other, though, and seldom held a grudge. I tried never to get between them. Although my grandmother loved me more than life itself, she could not be trusted to take my side against Rose if we should tangle on any issue.

When my grandmother died, I was the one giving orders. No one was to be let into the house until I got there, and then, the funeral director would come pick her up. There was to be no viewing, according to my grandmother's wishes. Somehow Rose got the news of Grandma's death very quickly — she had "spies" everywhere. When I arrived at the house, I was informed that Rose had already been there, defied my orders, and said a prayer over my grandma's dead body. There was no getting between those two. It took a while, but I eventually forgave Rose this transgression.

The bonds that tied Grandma Elvira and Cousin Rose together were formed long before I was born. I could see them but not understand what they were truly made of. I was simply doomed to be sucked into my genetic disposition of inheriting many of their traits. I have proven, though, that I'll never be able to boss the masters.

I often say that genetics is a funny thing — probably because ninth grade biology went mostly over my head. My second attempt to grasp the basic concepts of biology, in college, was also a dismal failure. Maybe that is why it has taken me most of my first forty years on this planet to recognize the role genetics plays in my life. Honestly, I probably figured that out in the first twenty-five and spent the last fifteen looking for a way to escape some of my genetic predispositions.

Whether by nature or by nurture, you are who you are. The challenge of life is to maintain a healthy balance between acceptance and change. This is perhaps an eternal struggle within the family. How much do you appreciate the traits you share and how important is it to you as an individual to standout? When do you create your own identity and what consequences might you face for trying to be different?

Becoming an adult, as I am just getting around to doing at forty, means looking at the family in a different way and trying to define for yourself your role in it. In an Italian family like mine, your value as a member is greater than your value as an individual. Constraints such as this are important to recognize and overcome to actualize your adult identity. I've defined the struggle, but am still working on how much I dare to disappoint my ancestors.

Tradition is Bittersweet — Minus the Sweet

Since I thought I grew up in this idyllic middle class family, relating to my grandparents and learning the family traditions, it makes sense on some level that I would try to re-enact the glory days by continuing the traditions. As I reached my early twenties and realized life was changing, I wanted to hold tight to those childhood memories. It has taken every moment of my first forty years to understand that some things just can't be duplicated.

When I was growing up, we had wonderful Christmas celebrations. I would look forward to Christmas for months. All four of my grandparents would come to stay with us. My father would take us to pick out a Christmas tree. Mom would make eggnog to drink while we trimmed the tree. My sisters and I would spend a whole day baking cookies under my mother's watchful eye. We would dress up for Christmas mass. We opened presents in our pajamas all-together on Christmas morning. Then, the mimosas would mark the beginning of a big holiday breakfast. Christmas was an ideal family event at our house, served up on the good china.

In my early twenties when I was first married, I took on the responsibility of hosting the Christmas festivities. Since my mother died a couple years earlier, Christmas hadn't been quite the same. It was time to reconstruct the big family Christmas and put those great memories back together. Plus, now I had a whole other family to fold into the fun. Wouldn't my in-laws be excited to see me host a traditional Christmas celebration?

At Thanksgiving, I made it clear to my family and my in-laws that I would be hosting a big combined family Christmas, and then the rumblings started. My two sisters-in-law had developed a schedule before I came into the picture, so that neither one had to spend two Christmases in a row with their parents. Naturally, one was on this year's schedule but the other planned to be with her in-laws (whom she honestly liked better).

Ok, so it wouldn't be the whole family at my house, but it would be close. My father would bring my grandparents. My sisters would both attend. My one sister-in-law would come with her family for the day. And, of course, my in-laws would make arrangements to be there. It was going to be a house full, just like Christmas is supposed to be.

I spent the next month stripping six layers of paint off the wainscoting in my dining room and listening to "suggestions" being phoned in for the impending holiday festivities. It seems everyone had her own picture of how a proper Christmas celebration should go. I had to import food from other states to fill all of the delicacy requests, "You know, it wouldn't be Christmas without pickled eel."

The last piece of wallpaper had hardly adhered to the dining room walls when my guests began to arrive. My in-laws were the bearers of our first Christmas present — an antique chandelier for the newly redecorated dining room. A welcomed gift, had they arrived three days earlier. The dining room had to be broken down to install the new fixture immediately to show my gratitude. That was an hour I hadn't planned on losing. Everything ran behind schedule after that.

When my sister arrived, I just looked at her with this look that must have said, "rescue me". She put me in the car and sped off to the nearest liquor store, coining the term "ABC emergency" along the way. We had a couple other "ABC emergencies" that week, some luckily are too far gone to remember. When the pressure of pleasing the entire family got to be too much, she would look at me from across the room and say, I think we're about to have an "ABC emergency." We'd disappear for several minutes and return with our sense of humor intact.

During one of those "ABC emergencies," we talked about our mother. How did she do this? Was it this hard on her? How come we never knew how stressful the holidays were? Why did she keep doing it every year? The rose-colored glasses had fallen away for the first time. Our wonderful, magical family Christmases were a big pain in the ass! We had to wonder if we had been selfish children to not see all the stress these gatherings caused my mother.

The highlights of hosting my first family Christmas include the fully decorated tree falling over in the living room while we sang carols in the dining room, my in-laws getting drunk on Christmas Eve, but thankfully not falling over in my house (that, I'm sure would have resulted in a lawsuit we'd still be fighting to this day), my sister inventing the "ABC emergency," returning the chandelier to the antique store once everyone had left and then announcing the end of my marriage.

Today I would rate this as a success — the tree fell over but the in-laws did not. Score! It's taken me a full forty years and a lot of leg work, however, to gain this perspective on my world. When I was in my twenties, I couldn't figure out if I had failed family or if family had failed me.

What makes holidays fun and stressful at the same time is that they evoke memories of holidays-past. Vivid childhood memories haunt the present with that whiff of idealism. The first definition you learn becomes the rule against which all others are measured. So, like many others, I spent my early adult life consciously, or unconsciously, trying to recreate the perfect holiday celebrations of my childhood.

When I was a child, we spent most Thanksgivings with my mother's parents at their house in New Jersey. Sometime on Wednesday afternoon, my parents packed us into the car for the six-hour drive that would end with sleeping children being carried into the house and put to bed immediately.

The main event on Thanksgiving morning was watching the Macy's parade on the 19-inch console TV in the living room while grownups scurried around the tiny kitchen preparing dinner. Eight of us would cycle one at a time through the solitary bathroom to dress for dinner. The youngest usually emerged first in their holiday finest as we resumed our seats in front of the TV.

The dinner table stretched beyond the bounds of the tiny dining alcove into the living room and was packed with dishes, glasses, and food. At least two people remained standing while food was passed around the table because with everyone seated it was impossible to squeeze back into the kitchen. And then we ate, and ate for what seemed like hours.

It was at one of those Thanksgiving dinners that I first learned the meaning of indigestion. That year, when I got up from the table, I thought I would explode. There in the house of the original food pushers I was a big eater, but I had never felt that uncomfortable before. I didn't know what was wrong with me. No more could go in and nothing was coming out. My father suggested several laps around the house to work it off, determining I was too young to indulge in antacids with the others.

Eight people in a house with one bathroom and a tiny TV set, eating themselves into a coma, somehow created the ideal image of family holidays in my childhood brain. Thankfully, my brain has finally matured to understand that that is not a scenario worth repeating — ever! I have finally redefined Thanksgiving for myself to include more space, fewer people, less food, and a larger TV. If that isn't success by forty, I don't know what is.

What I realize now is that family holiday gatherings are impossible. We try to reenact our wonderful childhood memories, or the definition of holidays that was imprinted on our childhood brains, but we have the insight and baggage of fully-grown adults. Through forty years of family holiday experience, I've learned three lessons:

1. Wonderful childhood memories are meant to be shared. Take out the pictures once in a while and tell the stories to people who weren't there.
2. Unless you can fit into that red velvet dress Grandma made you when you were eight, you cannot have the same holiday experience again. Take some of the traditions you loved, mix them with your own ideas, and create a new holiday memory each year.
3. Large family gatherings have gone out of fashion, whether due to the distance between us or the cost of overfeeding everyone. Being with family for a holiday doesn't mean being with the whole family. Pick a few like-minded relatives or some you haven't seen in years

and plan to celebrate with them. It's easier to visit with the family in small groups.

If Family Is Not Harmonious Sunday Dinners, What Is It?

After the first forty years of life, I don't see my family as any more functional (or less functional) than any others. I have come to realize what family is, but more importantly, what it is not. Family is a great place to start, and it is simply made up of the people around you when you are young. The people who feed, clothe and shelter you until you are able to do so for yourself are your family. Along with providing those material needs, they teach through example one way to live, to love and to look at the world. With those basic ideas, you then go out into the world, learn other ideas, and ultimately build a life for yourself. Your family will always represent the backdrop of that life.

Family is a living and fluid entity. As you go through life, your family changes. Old members die; sometimes young members die. New people come into your family from time to time, changing its dynamic. You can't stop change, but you sure can waste a lot of energy trying. Family is not the yardstick by which to measure your life. You don't get extra points for looking just like that family on TV.

You are not somehow a less important person because someone always ends up crying in the kitchen after Christmas dinner, or one of your relatives is always too drunk to carve the turkey on Thanksgiving (even if it isn't the same relative every year), or your high school graduation is remembered as the time one grandmother insulted the other to which she replied, "say that again and I'll scratch your eyes out," before ordering Grandpa to take her home immediately, or you arrive at holidays with elated anticipation and leave feeling sad and dejected. If anything, these experiences bond me (I mean, you) with everyone else on the planet who has a family they still talk to. After forty years as a member of a family, what I've learned is that we all have the same family, and it is all wonderfully painful.

CHAPTER TWO

"The first step in finding people who are like you is understanding what you are like."

Bonding and Bondage Sound So Similar

Relationships, both platonic and romantic, seem to follow family in the list of basic human experiences. After all, they are just an extension of human interactions outside of the familial circle. Everyone seems to have relationships, some good and some not so good. Even the most anti-social among us can claim to have had at least one friendship. It would seem a safe assumption, therefore, that developing relationships is a natural act that doesn't require much thought.

I am proud to report that on the eve of my fortieth birthday, I am much better prepared to perform the "natural act" of developing relationships. I have learned many helpful lessons along the way and am confident I could have a few healthy friendships sometime soon.

Not Everyone Wants to be Your Friend

College was not a fun experience for me. At least, it wasn't what the media had led me to believe it would be. I didn't make life-long friends there or attend great parties, meet my future husband, or set out on an exciting career path. But I did learn a lot of painful, awkward social lessons that I am grateful for – mostly.

The first lesson to smack me in the face came from my third roommate freshman year. From the time I was old enough to read the Sunday Times (at least the magazine section) I was enamored with New York City. I spent hours dreaming about the glamorous life I would lead one day living and working in the fashion capital of the world, the center of the universe since the beginning of time. There was something about the City's gritty history that intrigued and beckoned me.

Much to the chagrin of my mother, a woman who grew up on the Lower Eastside of Manhattan, my focus was on getting to the City instead of getting a good education. I chose the college closest to the City that my parents would let me attend – still "Upstate" by many standards. Freshman year came, and I was moving closer to what I believed to be the birthplace of all civilization.

After things didn't work out with my first roommate, I had the good fortune of being transferred to a room with another freshman. When I learned she was from Brooklyn, I just knew it was kismet. I was sure we would get to be the best of friends. I would bring her home on weekends to meet my family, and she would bring me home to Brooklyn with her. I would learn more about the City from a real insider. I was about to have my first New York City friend.

I'm not sure if you could see the excitement on my shiny white face as I moved my stuff into the empty half of her room. If it was visible, all of her hall-mates saw it as they watched, hands on hips and heads bobbing side to side. The next morning when I inquired about the smell of bacon wafting down the hall, I was told Big Shaquita made breakfast for everyone. I was not invited. I was never invited to do anything with my roommate and her friends. They seemed to all come from the same neighborhood and spoke a sort of code I never could crack.

I was as open and friendly with all the girls on the hall as I knew how to be. They mostly walked in and out of my room as if they didn't see me. I showed interest in my roommate by asking her about her beauty routine and the products she used. You know, girl talk. I watched her use the curling iron, and seeing the freshly made curl stand right where the iron left it, expressed my desire to have hair that did that. She told me nappy hair was nothing to wish for.

In the end, she won. I couldn't take the isolation any longer and requested to be moved to a different room. For months after that I could not understand why that nice black girl from Brooklyn didn't want to be friends with me. After all, racism was supposed to work in the other direction. If I were ok with her, why wouldn't she be ok with me? I had no problems with her. I really wanted to get to know her. Why didn't she want to have anything to do with me?

That experience stung for a long time. It was the first time I realized there are places in this world where I am not welcome. I thought I was this sophisticated, worldly teenager when in fact I knew very little about the world outside my neighborhood. I didn't even realize that there was a very different world out there full of people who weren't all just waiting for me to reach out to them in kindness and friendship. I had no idea that everyone didn't share my curiosity about everyone else and that being nice wouldn't automatically win me friends.

Looking for Friends in all the Wrong Places

It wasn't until after college that I really understood that you have to go out of your way to make friends. It took me even longer to realize that the people who have the greatest potential to be your close friends are those who are like you in many ways.

I always wanted to meet people who were different, who had different backgrounds, different upbringings. I wanted to learn new things, new ways of seeing the world. That's what sending me to a liberal arts college got my parents, a daughter who decided it was a good idea to sample the world rather than stick with what has worked for us for generations.

I enjoyed school, got along well with my teachers and got good grades. My parents, being educators, always managed my education. They chose my classes and in some cases my teachers. They set high standards for me while taking the responsibility for academic decision-making out of my hands. They knew best.

When I went off to college it was my turn to make those decisions. I was tired of the core academic curriculum and wanted to branch out. Wasn't college the place to try different things and find yourself? I signed up for horseback riding, psychology, drawing, and guitar. It took my parents three semesters to convince me to try an English class (that was their/ our core discipline.)

I met people who were different from me, all right. While I learned a lot about the world and myself, I did not make friends. Turns out that there is a difference between tolerance and friendship. And in some situations, curiosity might not come across as friendship, either. It was many years after college when I finally took this lesson home. After years of experimentation with relationships and differences, I finally got it. You want to come "home" to someone who is just like you and that's ok. All those "different" people do the same.

Cultivating Sameness

The first step in finding people who are like you is understanding what you are like. I realize now on the eve of my fortieth birthday that knowing myself is the basic key to developing relationships.

Of course, I always thought the emphasis was on getting to know other people. Turns out, you have to know yourself and be able to project a clear image of that self to others. Other people are all looking for people they recognize to befriend. If they can't figure out where you fit in, they're probably not going to make the effort.

Here are some ideas I've developed about how to define your own personality and express it in the world so similar beings can find you.

- Figure out what you like to do and devote some time to doing it. Writers write. Musicians make music. Athletes train and compete. Pick one thing you enjoy and actually pursue it, don't just dabble. It doesn't have to end up defining you completely, but it will give you a base to work from.

- Pick a signature drink - even if it's club soda, although I can't believe anyone really likes that. Consistency is how we define ourselves, to ourselves and then to others. Decide what you like and stick to it for a period of time – like years. If you decide to change it in the future, you can refer back to this as your "club soda phase."

- Embrace some part of your heritage and incorporate it into your definition of yourself. I am a New Yorker. I've lived in various regions of the state and truly appreciate the culture here — it is a part of me.

- Clarify your visual expression of yourself, and then represent that look consistently. Whether your style is classic, preppy, Goth, athletic, or something no one has labeled yet, own it. Once adolescence is over, the experimenting is done. Pick the look you like best for yourself and stick with it.

If only I had learned sooner that I had to define myself before I could have meaningful relationships, I might not have wasted so much energy at the bar every night trying to decide what drink to order. While my first forty years were spent fighting routine, working hard to defy definition, I think the next forty will be easier with a clearer vision of myself projected to the world.

When Making Friends Was Easier

I was never the most popular girl in school, but I always had a handful of friends. Even though I attended three different high schools in four years, I managed to find someone to eat lunch with most of the time. These were the people I called friends and whose status as such made me feel socially acceptable.

What I later realized was that those were the people who had the same lunch schedules as me. The friends I had during grade school were almost by default. They were the kids whose last name started with the same letter as mine, the ones who were assigned the seat next to mine in chorus, and the kids who lived in my neighborhood and rode the same bus as me.

Simply walking from my dorm room to class and back everyday did not win me any friends. It never occurred to me that I would have to get involved in an activity or club if I expected to make friends. Maybe even initiating interaction with others outside of class would help. Nope, I was never a joiner, therefore, seldom met people with the same interests as I had.

As I came to understand a bit too late, you have to make an effort to make friends. Friendships do not just sprout up out of nowhere because you are "good" or "nice." The good and nice don't necessarily find each other and stick together.

The first step is to engage in activities that interest you. That's where you find people you have something in common with. (If you don't understand the importance of that, re-read the previous section of this chapter.) Joining a club or volunteer organization is a good start. Taking a class can help, too, but then you have to reach out to people.

In my early twenties, I thought making friends was about making yourself likable (perfect). My hair was never out of place; my shoes always matched my outfit (and each other); my manners were impeccable. I knew which fork to eat with; I always used a napkin. I couldn't figure out why I never made new friends.

My ex-husband was a great conversationalist. If we were at a party, he could talk to a post and it would think it was having a good time. I observed his behavior very carefully. When he met a stranger, he repeated his name often in the conversation. He would ask those stupid questions I never bothered with, like what do you do? What do you think about this weather? Did you hear what the President said about nuclear disarmament?

I, on the other hand, would meet a stranger at a party and begin by forgetting her name. Of course, I would be too embarrassed to admit it, so I would stumble through the conversation hoping she didn't notice. My bluff became really awkward if someone tried to join the conversation and I wasn't able to make the introductions.

The extent of my conversational abilities was asking your name and your occupation — sometimes in rapid-fire succession and sometimes I would space my questions out. I didn't keep up on current events, so that was not a good subject to raise. If someone else raised it, I would make an excuse like I had been too busy to watch the news that day.

I never asked any clarifying questions because I didn't want anyone to know I didn't know what they were talking about. Someone could tell me he worked as a futures commodity trader, and I would smile and nod as if I knew everything about that profession. After all, how was I going to make new friends if people thought I was stupid?

I am happy to report that somewhere along the way to my fortieth birthday I came to realize that conversations are built on stupid questions. If you show an interest in what someone does or says, she is more likely to continue the conversation. Eventually these inane discussions of the weather, travel routes, or mundane occupations lead to more in-depth human interaction, which can lead to friendship. Who knew? (Everyone but me, apparently!)

Here are some random lessons on making friends that I hope to employ in my forties:

- Seek out friends; don't wait for them to come to you. Take the initiative to suggest meeting for coffee, lunch, or a walk. The person will either become your friend or move out of town and change her name. Either way, at least you tried.

- The most likely friends are people with whom you have things in common. Join a club, take a class, and get involved in your community. Do the things you enjoy in a public space where others can join you.

- You don't have to act smart; if you're smart they'll figure it out. Successful friendships usually take place between people of similar intelligence. Through basic conversation, these things will sort themselves out. If you start out putting on airs, you'll be exhausted before the initial bonding phase is completed.

- Asking questions is the easiest way to initiate conversation, which is how friendships begin. Weather and traffic conditions are usually two safe bets. Instead of thinking you're boring for talking about the weather, the other person will likely feel relieved that you broke the ice, so she doesn't have to.

The Myth of Best Friend Status

When I was in third grade, I met the girl who was to become my best friend. From third grade until her family moved out of town in seventh grade, Patty and I were inseparable. We rode our bikes together, listened to music, made up dance routines, rode the same bus to school, styled each other's hair, and shared clothes. Everyone knew we were best friends.

When Patty moved away, we maintained a letter-writing campaign to each other that lasted through high school graduation. We continued to share all the intimate details of our lives like any other teenage girls, and there was the occasional weekend visit. As we grew up, we shared our thoughts and ideas about everything from music to boys. We made plans to take road trips together when we were older and to be in each other's weddings.

After high school, Patty and I went in different directions. We kept in touch but we would never be as close as we were growing up. Eventually, we had a terrible falling out over a boy, of course, that ended our long-standing friendship. I was angry over what I perceived to be her horrible offense against me, a breach of loyalty. She couldn't understand why my loyalty to someone else seemed to come before her. As time went on, I was lost without my best friend.

I realized what a grounding force having a best friend had been for so many years. Years after the break-up I tried to figure out what really went wrong. What I discovered was that Patty and I had grown apart. For the last couple years of our friendship we didn't enjoy common experiences anymore. The changes in our lives seemed to reveal differences in our interests and shaped our perspectives on the world.

She wasn't the only old friend I lost for that reason. I seemed to hold on to friendships out of habit. Long after there was any basis for a friendship, I counted certain people among my friends because they had been for so long. I think I was afraid to give up the old ones because I wasn't really making any new friends.

Old friends who knew you when you were growing up felt like the only true friends. Those who had come along later felt more like acquaintances. Without those old, true friends, I felt like nothing at all, as if I needed them to legitimize my existence. But when their goals and values became (or revealed themselves to be) so different from my own, I risked a different type of identity crisis.

Risk was always a great way to describe my friendship with Suzan. We bonded in high school because we both existed on a similar fringe of the social scene. She was older and faster than I was, but we concentrated our friendship on our common interests in clothes and music.

At the end of our friendship fifteen years later, I had to choose between the loyalty of friendship and self-preservation. Suzan did something wrong, got herself into legal and financial trouble, and then did a series of terrible things to try to recover. When I figured out what she was up to, I wrestled with the idea of giving up on a friend.

I sympathized with her situation (which despite all her protests she had created herself). But in the end I realized I would never have done what she did. Her behavior revealed a difference in our core values that I could not live with or even associate with any longer. (Funny how my mother knew many years earlier that Suzan was bad news and always tried to keep some distance between us.)

What I've learned is that having a best friend only offers false status. What's really important is the quality of your friendship, not the longevity of it. Chances are pretty good that no one person will be able to meet all of your needs and expectations as a best friend for life. Some people have this, but on closer examination they might admit at times it is in name only.

Instead of looking for the perfect friend, you have to look at people for who they are and how you can connect with them. The friend you met in choir practice is probably the one you call to go over a new piece of music, but she may not be the one you confide your diet cheats to. Your married friend may not be the person you share your man-hating rant with, but she is definitely the one you call to borrow a dress for that special date.

A friendship does not have to exist on every plain. That is the wisdom of having more than one friend. Each person connects with a certain part of your personality or intersects your life at a particular point. You should think of friends more like accessories, people who add sparkle to your life, and less like undergarments, items you don't dare leave the house without.

Lessons about best friends:

- They don't make you who you are. You have to define yourself and continue to act on your beliefs, no matter what your friends think. Sometimes that means separating from a friend on a particular issue, for a short time, or permanently.

- Best friend is not a title for life. Best friends can fall from grace or simply move on in different directions. You should be careful how you throw superlatives around, anyway. Stick with good friends because you can have many of those.

- Having friends who don't share your core values is worse than not having friends. In the extreme, you run the risk of compromising your values simply by condoning the bad actions of a so-called friend.

- When you let someone into your life deep enough to be your best friend, you make yourself vulnerable to that person. People are not perfect, and friendship doesn't exist without a level of vulnerability. Try to balance your risk with the potential reward.

More Than Just Friends

As luck would have it, one's friendship skills, or lack there of, tend to spill over into romantic relationships, as well. In hindsight, my deficiencies in this arena were predictable but somehow not avoidable. While I was busy focusing on all the romantic ideas I gathered from the movies, no one bothered to tell me I was doing it wrong. Or, if they did, I couldn't hear them.

Did you ever meet someone who was a great first date? That was me. I looked the part, dressed well, and was very polite. I could easily order off of any style menu, liked all types of food, knew enough about wine to pronounce my favorite flavor, and could smile through the most mundane chitchat. It was all downhill after the first date, however, because I really thought the work stopped there.

Boys don't want to date girls who don't clean their plates. At least that's what my parents taught me. (Yup, Dad was in on this one.) Some girls internalize this message as permission to over eat and get fat; however, I took it to mean that I should be hyper concerned about making boys like me. Once again, I set out on my quest to make myself perfect because I thought that if a boy liked me, my life would be magical.

It took me many years and several horrible relationships to realize that the boy was not the only one who got to choose. A boy liking me was only half the equation. I also had to like him, and it was ok to turn down the ones I didn't like. The problem was that I was so focused on my behavior (looking and acting like the "perfect" date) that I seldom noticed their flaws, until it was too late.

I once managed to control my gag reflex through an entire meal with a pre-med student who described in detail the first surgery he scrubbed in on. I smiled sweetly all evening and couldn't understand why there was never a second date. I couldn't see that he was doing me a favor by not pursuing a relationship. Then, there was the law student who could not stop talking about himself, the entrepreneur who told me what he paid for everything, and the college dropout who made up stories about his success.

Somewhere in my first forty years, I finally realized that I get to decide who is worthy of my time and attention. I owe it to myself not to waste my time and energy on someone who doesn't meet my standards. I need to be less focused on what I have to give and more focused on what I need to get out of a relationship.

On the eve of my fortieth birthday I finally understand that making boys like me is not the basis of a healthy relationship. Just as important as being likable is being discerning about the qualities in your mate. If he has poor manners, is mean or just isn't too bright, he might not be the right person for you. No matter how blue his eyes are, you can't make it work with someone who just isn't your proper match. It is fair to expect good things in return for all the good qualities you offer.

Of course, relationships are more than just choosing the right partner. What I've learned in forty years is that it takes a lot of work to have a healthy, fulfilling relationship. Part of this conclusion I'm extrapolating, of course, because I haven't achieved that yet. I have gained some insights, however, in my own do-it-wrong-and-learn sort of way.

- If you don't know what you want from your own life, you won't be happy living it with someone else. A good relationship requires two strong individuals who maintain their own personal goals in life.

- Shared goals do not mean that you will become a successful professional and I will iron your shirts. While there are some tasks at which partners take up a dominant and subordinate role (we can't all be the foreman) the main goals must be shared equally.

- When you get married, your primary loyalty moves to your spouse. This is now the person with whom you make decisions and who's support and understanding is most necessary. Whoever was your primary confidante before, whether it was your mother or your best friend, has to take a backseat to your spouse.

- Compromise is an important ingredient in a healthy relationship but it is also a delicate balance. Being a dishrag and giving in to the other person's desires every time does not make a good relationship. Compromise has to go both ways.

- Anger happens. You have to feel it to get past it. But if you throw it at your partner, someone will get hurt.

- Trust is to be protected at all times. What he doesn't know can hurt him, and you, and the relationship.

- No one is a perfect communicator; everyone needs to improve. The things that are hardest to talk about are the ones that matter the most. Learning and practicing good communication habits is a life-long pursuit that can lead to a healthy relationship.

When Dating Turns to Mating

Here's a bit of logic I picked up along the way: if the relationship isn't good to begin with, it isn't going to blossom into great marriage material. I guess it just goes back to being more discerning about whom you spend your time with. If dating a man has some serious ups and downs, why would you want to lock yourself into it for life?

At this juncture I am still trying to figure out the whole purpose of marriage. I spent so much time assuming that it was my destiny that I never bothered to consider why. It was just something that everyone did, and I was not planning to be an exception to the rule.

My parents and grandparents seemed to enjoy marriage, and it was what they expected of me. It became what I expected of myself and seemed to be at the root of all adult life. We didn't know any couples who lived together but weren't married. I don't recall any single parents when I was growing up. If parents were divorced, it was a long time ago and they had quickly re-married.

One year I got a job doing in-home childcare for a somewhat precocious toddler. She was the only child at the time of two college professors. Several months into the job, I got engaged and weddings became a frequent topic of conversation. Her bag of library books included a book about a wedding, which she liked to read over and over. She knew that I was going to be a bride.

During one of our wedding conversations, Annie asked me why people got married. For a few seconds I was completely stumped. I could have given her the standard Catholic answer (I think), but I took my job very seriously and believed it did not include passing my own values along to someone else's child. As the child's daily companion and caregiver, I was a stand-in for her parents and as such should communicate their values to her.

We had already covered the fact that Annie's parents had had a wedding before she was born. Her mother was a bride who flouted convention in a red dress, and their ceremony took place at a country inn with a small group of family and close friends. I also knew that Annie's parents lived together for several years before they were married.

As I scrambled to come up with an answer to Annie's question that fit her parents' scenario, although I had never had such a philosophical discussion with them, it came to me. I told her that people got married in order to have children. She bought it and we continued reading books. Later her mother confirmed that answer to be perfectly acceptable for her moral framework.

The truth is, I didn't know why people got married. I certainly didn't know why I was getting married other than it was the next thing to do in life. If I had been spontaneous, I would have told her that when people love each other they get married. But that wasn't a real answer. People don't get married every time they fall in love, and marriage is not a prerequisite to continued love, in fact sometimes it turns out to be a deterrent, but that's another book.

After forty years of life, the purpose of marriage remains a mystery to me. I still believe in the concept and the social convention of it, but I cannot cite the purpose. In my experiences so far I can't say that I'm happier being married than being single. Somehow a happy marriage remains a goal of mine, although I am not really sure why.

Despite Best Intentions, Divorce Happens

From this vantage point it is easy to see how divorce happens. But when I was younger and first married, I never expected it to happen to me. I never gave it much thought at all, in fact. I took those marriage vows to be permanent...but then being married was not the great emotional apex I thought it would be.

I spent fourteen months planning my wedding. We got engaged on Christmas morning and were married the following February. Looking back, I should have heeded my father's warnings that a long engagement was not a healthy way to start a marriage. But since I've only recently learned the value of parental advice (see chapter one) I persisted.

The reason for the long engagement was all about wedding plans. I refused to be married in the summer because of my distain for pastels. All of the summer fabrics and colors are wrong for me. My perfect wedding would take place in the colder weather with rich, heavy fabrics, long sleeved gowns, and a deep color palate.

After we settled on a date, I threw myself into creating the perfect wedding. I knew I'd have to work extra hard because my mother wasn't around to help me. Actually, my mother would have reeled me in a bit and helped me focus on something more important, the marriage.

I worked, and studied and researched to plan every detail of the wedding. Not only did I design my wedding dress, but also I orchestrated pre-wedding social interactions between the groomsmen and the bridesmaids. I had never undertaken a project so big in my entire life, but I was good at it. I thought through every detail.

And with all of the energy I poured into wedding plans, I never gave the marriage one thought. It never occurred to me that the day after the wedding was going to come, all the festivities would be over, the guests would go home, and my life would be changed forever.

I might as well have believed I was going to live the rest of my life in that big white dress that was custom made from Italian silk for all the attention I gave it. After fourteen months of planning and assuming the role of bride-to-be, I was not prepared to be anything else. My post-wedding life had no purpose; I felt lost, alone, and directionless most of the time.

Years after the marriage ended, my precious wedding dress, carefully preserved in a fancy box, succumbed to water damage and mold in a basement flood. I cried when I realized it could not be salvaged. Truthfully, some of the tears were for the life it represented that had succumbed to reality in my mid-twenties.

The Anti-Wedding

In the first couple years after my divorce, I worked as a banquet waitress at a golf course that did a swift summer wedding business. I came in early to set the tables with hundreds of dollars of decorations and wedding favors that someone thought were necessary and precious. Sometimes the bride or her mother would stop by to give explicit instructions about how to place the candy bars with the customized labels or the little plastic bottle of bubbles.

I wanted to explain to those people that no one cared how the table was arranged. No one would remember what trinket was given as a wedding favor. Many of them would end up on the floor or in the trash, if not here later that night, the next morning at someone's house as they emptied their pockets before sending the suit to the dry-cleaners.

Someone needed to tell these people that they had wasted hundreds of dollars on plastic decorations that no one would remember or care about. That money could have been spent on the couple's first month's rent, groceries, gas for those visits home, or anything practical. Mostly they needed to know that a perfect wedding didn't make a good marriage.

Standing in the back of the dining room, during that lull between serving dinner and cleaning up, I watched blissful young couples celebrate with their families and friends and I realized I had become cynical about weddings. The joyful purpose I had found in every minute detail of my wedding was wiped away by the failure of the marriage.

This was a sad way to learn a lesson, but I continue to be a hands-on learner in life. No longer cynical or bitter, I sum up the wedding experience this way:

- If you just want to have a party and wear a big dress, that's ok. Don't call it a wedding. Theme parties are always in fashion. Choose a theme that makes you feel like queen for the day and have a ball.

- Don't treat your wedding as a rite of passage. It's not time for you to get married until you can think beyond the tall cake and the first dance. When you think it would be more tragic not to share the rest of your life with your partner than it would be to walk down the aisle in pale pink tulle, then it might be time to plan a wedding.

- Wedding planning is big business because it consists mostly of emotional expenditures. If you can't be practical about the budget, bring along someone who can. For a wedding of 100 people, a five-dollar wedding favor will add $500 to the budget. Favors are a nice touch but make them practical and consumable. Your wedding may be the event of the season, but for your guests the glow won't last forever. They don't need a keepsake of your big event that lasts forever, either.

- The honor of being invited to your wedding shouldn't come with a financial obligation scarier than their first mortgage. When planning your wedding, think about what it will cost for your guests to attend in time, travel, attire, and gifts. It is your day, but that doesn't mean everyone else should suffer.

Society still builds up weddings as every little girl's dream. It's great to have a fantasy, something extraordinary that you daydream about. But fantasies are usually best kept in your imagination. Once you live the fantasy, the mystique is gone.

The most beautiful actual wedding day anyone could have would be one that was filled with love and happiness. The dress, decorations, menu, music...none of those things really make a great wedding. A great wedding is one that is followed by a long and happy marriage. The tallest cake in the world cannot make that happen.

It's not the Wedding but the Marriage

I had a pretty tall cake, and my marriage only lasted four years. Along with my romantic notions about the perfect wedding, I had some ideas about marriage – none of them practical. I expected marriage to last forever. To be fair, I also expected true love to last forever, and I was sure I had found true love.

I don't know what happened to love. I think it was still there; at least polite civility remained always. Love probably shifted from that hot burning passion you have in the early months of a relationship to a quieter more reserved glow. After all, no one has the energy to sustain such a passion long-term.

Somehow we grew apart in a very short time. I had looked forward to my married days as a time when I would always have a date for events and adventures. We had some adventures together, but mostly I was attending weddings alone. I seemed to spend a lot of time alone, much more than I anticipated a married woman would. Finally, the only solution I could see to my perpetual unhappiness was divorce.

Divorce takes on a new meaning when you are in it. I had always believed that unless your husband beat you, there was no good reason to get divorced. You had a chance and you chose the one you're with. Come what may, you have to live with it.

My situation was far less dramatic than that. I was just unhappy and refused to live the rest of my life that way. Even now it seems a little selfish. I talked with my husband about how I felt. We'd talk and things would change for a while, but we always ended up back in the same place.

I refused to be unhappy any longer, and somehow I thought not being married would solve that problem. We counted out the wedding china, each taking six place settings, sold the house and went our separate ways. It was a sad time.

I remember I cried the hardest when I thought about all the expectations I had for our life together. All those beautiful wedding gifts that were meant to help us entertain our family and friends in our new home together, plans to celebrate milestone anniversaries, the family heirloom highchair that would some day hold a real baby...

Those things would never happen. Our house was not the happy home I expected it to be. Twelve place settings of matching china and separate glasses for red and white wine were useless when the marriage came apart. The trappings were all part of the fairytale, which couldn't sustain itself in the real world.

I never thought I would be divorced, but there I was in my late twenties when it happened to me. For the longest time I couldn't stand to admit I was divorced. The sound of it made me feel old and discarded, and I carried a heavy burden of shame.

Plus, I was in mourning. No matter how amicable a divorce is, it has the dull ache of loss and the stench of failure and disappointment. I was grateful my divorce didn't measure up to some of the horror stories I heard. There were no orders of protection or pit-bull lawyers involved.

My ex-husband volunteered to paint the kitchen in my new house, and we remained friendly for several months. But I watched him growing into someone I didn't know, and eventually it felt surreal to think that I had been married to this man. I wondered if I had kept him from realizing himself, this new self I didn't really like, and I tried to look at the divorce as the best thing for both of us.

At Least the Pain Brings Lessons

Divorce is a complicated matter that unfortunately becomes a reality for many people. Trying to date in my thirties, I discovered that most of the available prospects are divorced. I used to think that divorce was a red flag, that something was wrong, but I've come to understand that every story is different. I've learned a few intimate lessons about divorce:

- Even loving, well-intentioned people get divorced. It isn't a sign that they are not marriage material. It just means the particular combination didn't work.

- Divorce could mean you made a choice very early in life that no longer fits your lifestyle. People grow and change; sometimes that's the good news. It can be more merciful to go your separate way than to try to drag an unwilling spouse along with you.

- No matter the reason for the divorce, it still hurts everyone involved. Families that were thrown together are pulled apart. Friends choose which spouse to remain loyal to. Some can't handle the awkwardness and just fade away.

- Divorce is not just the failure of a marriage, or the end of love. It can also be a personal triumph over pain or mediocrity. There can be true inner strength displayed in making the decision to walk away, the kind of strength that, if discovered earlier, could have prevented the whole disastrous marriage from happening in the first place.

- Divorce, like mourning, should be treated with kindness. No matter what the circumstances, it is an emotionally vulnerable time that only the two people involved can truly understand. The rest of us should only offer gentle support and never criticism or judgment. As my mother would say, M.Y.O.B. (mind your own business).

Ways to Make Marriage a Viable Option

While I didn't spend much of my childhood dreaming of my wedding, I did have certain expectations. Of course, I would get married someday in a big white dress. My marriage would bare children, my new family would in many ways resemble the family I grew up in, and we would all live happily together forever.

Not a bad dream but it didn't happen that way. After years of analyzing the situation, I realize it was all my fault. I had a dream, a vision really, of what my life would be, but it was based on a child's view of the world and I had no plan to make it happen. I was just skating along through life with expectations, about as realistic as a young girl kissing toads.

My poor dating skills turned into poor mating skills partly because I wasn't prepared to do my part in the selection process. Since I expected to have children one day, and my assumption was that I would be married to their father at the time of conception, I should have been vetting potential mates by their fatherhood skills.

Instead, I was "playing dress up," going on dates to enjoy the food, and basking in the glow of attraction. That might be a fine attitude for casual dating, but for someone who was motivated to find a husband, someone who had rather specific expectations, it was awfully lackadaisical.

Unfortunately, on the eve of my fortieth birthday I cannot report that I have marriage figured out. I have, however, dealt with a few misconceptions and have some ideas about how to make it work in the future.

- Forget about true love. Sure, love is real and an important component to a successful marriage, but it can also keep you from making a practical decision. Love doesn't pay the bills, clean the bathroom, or ensure he won't tell that embarrassing story in front of your boss.

- Do your due diligence. Check him out; ask around. You don't have to go into a relationship blind in this age of social media. Find out something about this guy other than what he is telling you.

- Talk about goals. There is no point in getting involved with a man who doesn't like kids if you expect to have a big family. Be sure your basic life goals align before getting too involved.

- Don't ignore the warning signs. If you don't feel comfortable with the way he treats people or how he spends money, walk away. These habits are indicative of a value system that doesn't fit with yours. You can't change him, but you could die trying.

- Be honest with yourself. Ultimately, you are responsible for your own happiness (see chapter five). No matter how wonderful the man in your life may seem, he is not the reason for the sunrise. Don't blame him for the cloudy days.

- Keep your expectations realistic. No matter how dreamy he is, marrying a man won't change who you are. If you are lucky, work hard, and choose wisely, it may enhance your life, but even the best relationship doesn't include a lot of tall cakes.

CHAPTER THREE

....

"I cried ... I cried because I felt sorry for myself because I couldn't stop crying."

....

Compassion with a Side of Baked Ziti

I can remember my understanding of death as a very young child. I was only about three years old when the concept was mentioned, probably in the context of normal cognitive development. I visualized myself in death as floating in the blue sky away from everything and everyone.

That visualization went along with a dull emotional feeling of nothingness. I actually felt an abrupt end to everything. Even now, almost forty years later, I can remember that vision and recreate the feeling. I've learned since then, however, that it is not really that simple.

Like everything else, the lifecycle develops more meaning as you experience it. One day I was just like everyone else, living my life with a family that included all four of my grandparents alive and well. Then, all of a sudden I'm about to turn forty and death has reduced my family by three grandparents and one parent. I feel lonely and scared, my support system greatly eroded.

When we think about death, we usually think about our own death. The fear of the unknown, the anxiety of unfulfilled goals, and the pain of grieving loved ones make a contemplation of your own mortality difficult. But experiencing the loss of others begins to put life and death into a different perspective. You suddenly realize how fragile your relationships are and how quickly life can turn into something you never imagined.

My grandmother confided to me once that when she was young, she used to hug and kiss her mother every chance she got. (Grandma was born in 1905 the youngest of seven children to an immigrant family, so I'm sure she had to stand in line.) "I loved her up," she said, "because I knew I wouldn't have her forever." I don't know where Grandma got this wisdom about life, but she was right. One of the few consolations I had when she died at 98 was that I had "loved her up" every chance I got.

First Brush with Death

When I was about 10 years old, my dog died. I had never experienced the pain of loss before. I came home from school one day and Daisy wasn't around. My mother told us that she was at the vet. Over dinner, she explained that when she backed her car out of the garage, she heard Daisy whimper in the driveway. (Poor Mom thought she had run over the dog.) She jumped out of the car, scooped up the dog and headed straight to the vet's office.

When she got there, they determined that Daisy had had a stroke and kept her for treatment. The next day as I was walking home from the bus stop, my sister's little friend came running up and blurted out that Daisy was dead. Mom confirmed a call from the vet saying Daisy would not recover the use of her hind legs. Mom thought it would be too cruel to see her suffer like that and told the vet to go ahead and put her down.

I cried over that dog every day for a week. I cried because I missed playing with her. I cried to see the empty spot on the floor where her bed had been. I cried to think of what pain she must have endured. I cried for the anxiety she must have felt knowing something was wrong but not understanding what was happening to her. I cried because I felt sorry for myself because I couldn't stop crying.

My mother held me and explained over and over how it was best this way. There was nothing we could do for Daisy. No one could have seen this coming. Someday we'll get another dog, but we have to finish grieving for Daisy first. And finally, when you've cried enough, you have to try to think happy thoughts. It's not healthy to get stuck in a depression and just keep wallowing in it. Daisy's loss is sad but there are other things in life.

Try to Think Happy Thoughts

It's ironic that when my mother knew she was dying, she told me how lucky our family had been all these years. We had not lost a member to disease or accident. My grandparents were even still healthy in their old age. Other families had endured such tragedies, but we were whole, for now.

I moved home in September just after my 21st birthday, and my mother died of cancer the following July. I had nine months with her, six while she battled ovarian cancer and three as she succumbed to it. It goes without saying that losing my mother changed my life forever. But looking past the pain, it also taught me some life lessons I can be grateful for.

My mother was born with New York moxie, a fast walk, and a no-nonsense attitude. She always had a way of boiling issues down to their simplest form and finding a way to move forward. When I was stressed out, she would ask me what was wrong. In the dramatic way I inherited from my father, I would tell her, "Everything is going wrong!"

She'd calmly ask, "Like what? What is everything?"

So I'd tell her, "Well, there's this..." detailing the primary issue.

"Ok," she'd say, "what else? You said everything."

Believing that my first explanation didn't properly convey the severity of my life, I'd offer another example of something going wrong in my teenage world. My mother would briefly summarize my two explanations to prove she was following along and then ask for another.

"Ummm, I don't know, just everything," I'd sigh.

"I only heard two things. That's not 'everything.' Sounds like you need to adjust your perspective. Two things going wrong... you can handle that."

I invoke this strategy to this day in order to de-escalate my dramatic wind up to a bad day.

My mother handled the last nine months of her life with more grace, humility, and dignity than one could have expected from Mother Theresa herself. She was shocked, angry, determined, sad, and resigned, but most of all my mother was a teacher who showed us how to fight, hope, learn, accept, and make peace with life and each other.

I was with her the last time she checked herself out of the hospital. I think that was the day it sank in that she was not going to beat this disease. She was feeling rather well, and there was nothing more the doctors could do. It was time to get dressed and go home, which is where she really wanted to be. Of course, checking out of a hospital is like leaving a restaurant after a meal, suddenly everyone is too busy to complete your transaction.

This scene quickly became reminiscent of my childhood when my mother's New York moxie would embarrass me in front of friends, teachers, strangers...anyone who happened to be standing around when she decided it was time to stand up for herself – or me. Mom would grab me by the hand, march straight up to the front of the line, and loudly demand whatever I had been denied. The whole time I tried to disappear while insistently whispering, "it's ok, it's ok."

At the hospital that day I made one attempt to advocate for patience, but I could see Mom was at the end of her rope. I could just stand clear and watch as she marched out to the nurses' station and volunteered to sign any forms that needed to be signed before she left.

When she was urged to just wait until her nurse came into the room to check her out, she announced, "I do not have time to wait. This is the beginning of the rest of my life!" And out we went, Mom with hands on hips and me with head down frantically pushing the elevator button.

I didn't really get it that day, but as time went by I learned a lesson. I finally saw Mom's point in loudly standing up for herself. She wanted what she was entitled to, what she earned, what she had waited for. As a last resort, polite had to go out the window. What did they have her waiting for, anyway? There was no more treatment, she was healthy enough to walk, talk and wear regular clothes. Who was she hurting by creating her own schedule?

I wasn't embarrassed by my mother's behavior that day. I was proud of her for speaking up, and, honestly, I felt sorry for her. She knew her time was limited, and she wasn't willing to waste any more of it. I wish I had taken that lesson to heart that day. Instead, I spent the rest of my twenties and most of my thirties unable or unwilling to stand up for myself and take control of my life.

So this is a lesson half-learned in my first forty years — my life is my responsibility. I must diligently advocate for myself, especially since my mother isn't here to do it for me anymore. I understand the concept and accept its logic. Now, to implement... maybe in the forties.

The Rules of Mourning

Losing my mother was like losing a limb. For months after her death I still sensed her presence in the house. I expected to walk past her bedroom and see her lying there in bed, greeting me with a smile. Every now and then I thought I heard her cheerful hail coming down the hallway summoning someone to her room to impart the news of the day, or the moment. Some mornings I woke up early and went straight to her room as I had done for so many weeks, almost forgetting she wouldn't be there.

At first it was difficult to speak about her death. I called a couple friends with the news and asked them to spread the word because it was too painful to keep explaining over and over. And yet, there were moments when I wanted to shout it at passing strangers. I somehow needed people to know what had happened to me, what I was going through, maybe what I had survived, although it didn't feel like surviving at first.

For the first month I found some solace in the traditional mourning rituals. I hung a big black bow on the front door and dressed in black whenever I ventured out. Always the one to look the part, I actually found it comforting to express my grief this way. After thirty days, during a home visit our priest talked to me about the black bow. He felt it might be time for a white bow to symbolize Mom's entrance into heaven. I was in no humor to see the Catholic "bright side," but I conceded it was time to end the black mourning.

Mourning is a strange balance of public and private affair. Neighbors began to call with food and flowers almost immediately. (They probably heard Grandpa's periodic uncontrollable wails in those first several hours.) We graciously accepted their condolences, although some were awkward and uncomfortable. I remember greeting one neighbor as she carried her food offering to the kitchen. She began to cry and said she wasn't very good at this kind of thing. Her spontaneous vulnerability created a comforting bond.

Others who tried to do and say all the right things seemed contrived and unsympathetic. I'm often reminded of what my mother told me before she died when I complained about people saying stupid things to me about my mother's illness. She said, "Everyone is doing the best they can at any particular moment. If they could do any better, they would." That belief held me for quite a while and kept me from condemning those who appeared inept and uncaring.

I always call on those experiences when I console someone who is suffering a recent loss, and I remind myself that unless you've gone through something like this, you really have no idea what to do or say. The main goal is to be kind to anyone who is in great emotional pain. Some other good ideas I learned through this experience:

- Don't bring baked ziti. My family ended up with a freezer full of it. While it was kind that people brought food, and practical, since we really didn't feel like cooking for many days after the funeral, ziti became the cliché mourning food.

- Be present. Just showing up says a lot to people who are in mourning. There might not be anything for you to do, just be there. You can sit quietly, reminisce about the deceased, or listen to stories about those final days and hours. Human companionship can be healing.

- No one buys the "better place" argument, so save it. My mother's cousin went through an elaborate story about how god had a different plan for my mother and that she would be setting the table in heaven waiting for us to arrive for the meal. This insensitive woman might be singing a different tune now that she has lost her own mother, but back then she was full of nonsensical wisdom.

- Realize that you can't fix it. Death renders us all helpless, a condition which doesn't sit well with some. They rush around doing things they think will help. All the baked ziti in the world isn't going to solve this "problem." The problem is that someone is gone and not coming back. Time and tears are the only solutions, so try sharing those.

- After the funeral, everyone goes home and gets back to their lives and the grieving are left with their grief. These are the really dark days when a note, a visit, or even some food would really help. It's easy to feel resentful of all the mourners who came out for the festivities, the public displays of grief, but can't find the time to share a little of your private grief, days and weeks later.

Welcome to the Club

One of the lessons I learned about loss in my first forty years is also about camaraderie. When you lose someone close to you, it can be a very lonely feeling. There is a hole in your life dangling at the end of a strangely severed connection. You can't truly explain your feelings, the things you suddenly think about in the middle of the night, the way you now question your simple life routines.

I questioned the wisdom of friends bringing food to our house, although I knew it was a standard social convention. Didn't they know how much we like to cook and eat? And bringing Italian food I thought was really bizarre. I don't even like to eat at Italian restaurants because I was raised on homemade Italian food. You know, no one's sauce is a good as your Italian Grandma's – in my case, my Italian Grandpa's.

Why didn't people make us food that was their own specialty, something they made better than anyone else, something they made better than baked ziti — no really!

It wasn't until I experienced the pain and shock of loss that I understood how someone who enjoys cooking as a means of relaxation and socialization could be so affected by grief as to not be able to motivate toward the kitchen at all. The first day, the first several days, we had to be reminded to eat. This was completely foreign behavior in my family!

As it turns out, social conventions have their merits. Whether you know what you're doing or you're just following the rules, you can be sure you are providing some sense of comfort. I know this now, having been on the other side of the casserole dish.

I joined an unfortunate and exclusive club on July 25, 1992, the day my mother died. My cousin Eric went before me and ushered me in when it was time. Ironically, he was with me that day and brought me home to face my loss for the first time.

When I was in high school, my mother's cousin Hugh died of cancer leaving a loving widow and five children. One of the youngest of those children, Eric, is my age, and we have since become good friends.

I remember all of the events surrounding his father's death back in the 1980s. There was the family picnic Hugh instigated, gathering the upstate branches with the down-staters. This was my first introduction to the kids on that side of the family. I discovered a few cousins right around my age. Then, there was a wedding with great controversy about whether children should attend the reception. We all got dressed up for the ceremony, but we children had our own party that evening. I didn't attend the funeral, either. Like the wedding, it was not a place for children. Although I was a teenager, I did not feel slighted.

The cousins were reunited at the next family picnic, which had become an annual event, partly to honor Hugh's memory. Each year we formed different alliances based on age and attitude. One year I asked about Eric's absence from the festivities. Our other cousin, same age different parents, told me that ever since his father died Eric was in a perpetual bad mood. Not one to jump on that type of bandwagon, I left the comment alone.

This same cousin, the one with two healthy, living parents and a superior attitude, was waiting at my house with the rest of the extended family after my mother's funeral. As I pushed along through the crowd like some type of receiving line, I came to her. Her words to me were appropriate yet shallow. But suddenly I remembered her disparaging comments about Eric. At that moment it clicked with me that I had joined his club, and that people like this shallow dimwit would never understand. I braced myself to be the subject of one of her next pointed comments.

I have had the unhappy occasion to welcome others into the club. It's a sad affair punctuated by a look of recognition and slight glimmer of hope when I quietly exclaim some truth that only members of our club could know. One of the most comforting things in life is to realize that you are not alone. You are not the first or only person to experience the extreme grief you are dealing with.

The death of someone important in your life changes your perspective on everything. Finding others who have this same post-death perspective is like having a lifeline. When someone has had the same experience you have, there is so much you don't have to explain. Loss is one of the toughest parts of life to get through. Hanging with other survivors, people who are like you at least in one respect, adds a sense of camaraderie so you're not out there all alone.

What Does It All Mean

I'd like to be able to report that on the eve of my fortieth birthday I have discovered the meaning of life and death. Of course, if that were true I'd be writing a much different book — probably more serious and boring. What I figured out about the death of my mother is that you don't get over a loss like that but you do find a way to live with it.

I spent many hours trying to figure out why this happened to me. There must be a reason, and beyond that, some great purpose to it all. I am a logical person and like to think my way out of trouble. I couldn't find any reason to believe that my mother was better off dead. She had a great life so far; she really wasn't finished. And the pain of her cancer didn't seem that bad. She never expressed a desire to die rather than continue fighting.

I could never find any logic in me being left without a mother at twenty-one. It was actually illogical because Mom and I had recently healed our rift caused by my adolescence and were finally becoming friends and allies. Since her death I felt her with me often. I heard her voice and held her in my dreams, but

I didn't see how this was any improvement over her physical being. I could not figure out a reason for her death.

The best logic I could discover was in a book called, When Bad Things Happen to Good People, that explained we live in a random universe where storms, plagues, and earthquakes are not intentionally directed at us as punishment. This logic appealed to me because I know my mother was a good person, and I certainly never did anything so bad as to warrant my mother being taken away from me.

It was an exercise in letting go to accept that my mother's death by cancer was random. She didn't catch it nor did any of us do anything to deserve this fate. It just happened. We did everything possible to affect a better outcome, but the powers of nature are largely beyond human control. Things happen and all we can do is respond to them, try to gain some wisdom...and breathe deeply.

Finding the Wisdom in Loss

After the first big one, it starts to get a little easier, I guess, but you'll never learn to avoid the pain of loss. "I don't ever want to be on this planet without you, Bert." I said in one of those late night phone conversations that covered a bizarre range of topics. Bert was one of those friends I talked to intensely for a short period of time and then didn't hear from for months. In the midst of our latest conversation it had occurred to me that our fifteen-year age gap meant in all likelihood, Bert would die before me.

Luckily, Bert understood I was hyper-focused on death since my mother's death several months earlier. When you lose someone close to you, you suddenly become afraid of losing others. He assured me that someday we would be sitting in rockers on a front porch somewhere comparing stories about our grandchildren.

Finding myself in his region of the state a year or so later, I decided to stop by and say hello to my friend Bert. When I pulled up to his house, his wife was out cutting the grass. She pulled up alongside my car and shut the mower off. Through the open window I asked if Bert was around. She looked at me with such a blank expression that I reminded her I am Bert's friend who lives upstate.

"I know who you are," she said. "Bert died last Summer." I didn't know what to say first. I had a million questions in my head, and I was hoping to discover this was a joke. It wasn't funny, though, and Suzy wasn't a real jovial person. I was finally able to exclaim, "I didn't know. No one called me." In hindsight it was a stupid statement. Who was supposed to call me? Suzy who had just lost her husband or my friend who was dead?

Suzy told me Bert was cremated according to his wishes. She buried some of his ashes in the top of his parents' grave and sprinkled the rest in the local creek. That seemed like a more fitting place for Bert than a cemetery. He was part of that valley and loved to swim in the creek in the summer. I never knew Suzy without Bert. It was strange to think she would go on living in "his" house, in his valley with his view of the river.

One minute I was contemplating a visit with Bert, the next minute he was dead. The shock was devastating and left me feeling alone and abandoned. Although I didn't realize it at the time, it brought back the same fears I had when my mother died. Suddenly it was as if I was all alone on this planet without a friend, an ally; my biggest cheerleaders were gone. In that moment I could only focus on what was lost and didn't take stock in the people I had left, the ones who had held me together after my mother's death and who would hold me while I cried over my lost friend.

A couple months later fate provided some closure for me in Bert's mourning. Suzy died in that same creek where she had spread Bert's ashes. While babysitting her neighbor's kids, she took them to walk the trail along the creek like she had done many times before. One of the children slipped into the water, and Suzy jumped in to rescue him. They both drowned tangled in the weeds from the bottom of the creek.

It was a shocking tragedy, but my romantic side saw poetry to it, as if Bert had reached up from the depths of that creek and pulled Suzy down to join him so they would not be separated any longer. I can't bring either one of them back, so I just try to ease my mind to live with the reality.

I've learned to trust in the grief process. What at first feels like too much to handle eventually works its way around to be the source of some new strength. At first I felt afflicted by this knowledge so early in my life. Why me? Why should I spend the rest of my life mentally entangled in death, watching out for it, planning for it, not fully enjoying life with the realization that nothing was permanent?

Now I can see it as a means of creating insight into life and the human condition. If I had a choice, I'd take my mother back and live the rest of my life in ignorance. But, since that's not an option, I accept the knowledge and try to find practical ways to apply it, understanding that it does not give me incite into how to avoid death but rather how to live with it.

Death and pain are inevitable but should not be deterrents to life. The value that we receive from the people who become important parts of our lives is internalized. In that way, they remain with us even after they die. It is up to us to recognize they are there and to continue to enjoy the impact they have on us.

The hard part is making the physical break when it is time. Letting go of the connection to a special person and turning inward to visit with the part of them that will always be in you takes time, practice, and faith. It means believing in what that person brought to your life and believing in your own ability to carry it forward.

How You Know You're Not There

A few years after my mother's death, I attended a funeral for a much older relative who died unexpectedly. Although my grief was far from healed, I was walking around like the poster-child for gracious mourning, taking pride in my survival thus far. My sadness at the loss of my great-aunt was almost mitigated by my anticipation of communing with the extended family that had formed the core of the mourning throngs at my mother's funeral.

As I greeted family members following the ceremony with polite sympathetic expressions, I suddenly was overwhelmed. I couldn't hold back the tears, and apologetically exclaimed, "You'd think we would be better at this by now." What I meant was, I can't believe I'm crying like this. I buried my 48-year-old mother, so you'd think I could take this funeral with a grain of salt.

"Better at this?" Did I really think that through experience people learned not to cry at funerals? Does that even make any sense? Maybe I thought I had used up all of my tears on my mother. Or that my heart could measure out sympathy in appropriate doses based on some sort of emotional gage?

So I thought I was a pro. Turns out the people who are most controlled at funerals are the ones who have never experienced the loss of someone really close to them. The experience of loss doesn't make it easier to join the mourners. It actually makes it harder because it brings back the emotions of your own deep wounds no matter how old they are. That's a lesson I continue to relearn every once in a while.

Knowledge Gained

Knowledge is something I am usually proud of, but on this topic it brings me mixed feelings. If my mother hadn't died when I was 21, I don't think I would be taking stock of my understanding of life and death on the eve of my fortieth birthday. But here I am, and one thing I've learned in almost forth years is to accept myself and my life as it is.

When it comes to death, here are a few things I've learned:

- Live fully while you can. Say what you mean. Don't wait for a special occasion to express your feelings or to let the people in your life know how much you value them.

- Loss always hurts, even when it can be predicted. If you are lucky enough to prepare for the last day, do and say all you can. But don't be surprised when the end still hits you hard.

- Cry now or cry later. Denied grief catches up with you eventually. You might think that if you let yourself cry, you will never stop. Even the worst grief passes in time when you let it out.

- Talk about the people you've lost, how they influenced your life, and how their spirit, their energy, and their perspective continues to guide you in certain ways. Be the personification of your relationship and they are never truly gone from you.

- Loss is inevitable; no one lives forever. Not a bad idea to pay some attention to your own legacy. Figure out what you want people to remember about you and become memorable in that way. Express yourself.

CHAPTER FOUR

....

"I've come to understand that my self-esteem is a relationship between me and myself. Other people's opinions of me are not part of it."

....

It's All About the Self in Self-Esteem

Before I could really make any progress on figuring out self-esteem, I spent several years blaming my parents because I didn't have any. They somehow managed to supply me with new school shoes every year, a ten-speed bicycle when I turned nine, and trips to Disney and the Bahamas, but they couldn't squeeze in a little self-esteem?

By their own admission, my parents tried to provide me with the things I needed to succeed in life. Really?! You thought I was going to make it without a healthy self-image?

I began to learn about self-esteem when I had to, in my thirties when I realized I didn't really have any and that was derailing my attempts to live a normal, happy life. I spent years wondering what it would have been like to understand the importance of building self-esteem during my formative years when it was supposed to develop. Unfortunately, my awareness of my self-esteem issue corresponded with the blaming years.

I wasted precious time thinking self-esteem was this commodity withheld from me by amateur parents, (refer to Chapter One to see how the blaming years worked out) which put me into a real scramble to make progress on this issue before my fortieth birthday. I am happy to report, though, that I have figured out a strategy if not an end game for my self-esteem struggles.

What is Esteem, Anyway?

What's the big deal? I know I am an attractive, intelligent woman, so how can you say I don't have self-esteem. I thought it was all about knowing yourself and appreciating your strengths and weaknesses. Of course, if you've been reading this book from the beginning you know that I'm not big on appreciating weakness. In almost every aspect of my life, I've attempted to achieve perfection, or at least my version there of.

My acceptance of my shortcomings prior to my fortieth birthday mostly consisted of two physical flaws I have always owned up to. Since puberty I realized that I have a small chest. This reality sank in with me around the end of high school, but I decided to embrace it. You might think it is no big deal, and in fact, at this point in life it really isn't. But as a teenager just developing a sense of sexual identity, it was a noticeable deficiency.

By the time I reached my twenties it was clear nature was not going to fill out the disproportion evidenced by a two-inch discrepancy between my hip and chest measurements that favored the hips. Rather than focus on this flaw, I learned to wear clothing that visually made up for the disproportion and got on with my life. I never let that one (both of them, actually) detract from my confidence, a sign of good self-esteem, I thought.

A few years after I came to grips with that horrible, disfiguring reality of my human body, and gave up strapless dresses for good, I realized something else. Girls who have straight hair wish it were curly and vice-versa. I can remember admiring my friend Jody's spiral locks when she looked at me and cursed them. I didn't even understand her logic, but she told me she wished her hair was straight, her life would be much easier.

For a while during those formative years, which for me lasted until last week, I envied girls with curly or straight hair because mine was neither. I could comb my hair out straight when it was wet, but as it dried certain parts chose to poke in different directions. They didn't really curl; they just bent, making the overall look awkward and unpredictable. The result was the same with a short-layered haircut, only worse. Short layers on top of my head would actually stand up, or puff up, adding height but not in a good way. As the haircut grew out, the hairs bent in a different direction almost every day. There was no consistency of hairstyle for me.

Hairdressers were always telling me what beautiful hair I had. I couldn't understand it because I never thought it looked "right." I finally decided to stop fighting it and figure out how to work with it. I adjusted my perspective based on what the professionals were telling me: it's a rich dark color, it's thick and healthy, and it has a naturally shiny finish. By embracing my natural hair and ending my hair-envy, I thought I added one more building block to a healthy self-esteem.

Accepting my physical features as they are does not amount to healthy self-esteem, however. Upon deeper consideration, I realized that physical appearance doesn't necessarily build self-esteem. If it did, all the ugly girls would be home crying their eyes out. I've seen plenty of ugly girls out and about, so appearance can't be the key to self-esteem. (Neither is this cocky attitude.)

I've even discovered that all that time spent in front of the mirror applying make-up, curling hair, and looking for wrinkles does not detract from character but actually enhances it. When I was an adolescent, my mother discouraged time spent primping. She seemed to think that attention to appearance made women seem less intelligent. We should be using the majority of our energy for intellectual or academic pursuits and not be too concerned about our appearance.

Mom's point was well taken. We can assume that anyone who can carry on an entire conversation about curling her hair or the quality of her manicure doesn't have anything substantive to talk about. But I took this lesson to the extreme and thought it meant I should avoid spending time on myself.

What I've learned is that, like many things in life, it's not the outcome that matters, but the process. Spending time on yourself, trying different hairstyles, putting on make-up, or any of a hundred other activities that take place when a woman is alone in front of a mirror, helps create your relationship with yourself.

You don't have to talk about it at dinner parties, in fact most people would prefer if you didn't. But getting to know yourself on the outside is part of developing self-esteem, which is really just having a positive relationship with yourself. So, appearance matters but not for appearance's sake, who knew?

Did you ever look at a picture of yourself and not realize that's what you look like? I bet your friends think it is a good picture of you, but you don't agree. That's because they spend all day looking at you while you maybe see yourself for a few minutes in the bathroom mirror while brushing your teeth and then not again until you repeat the ritual before bed. Your image of yourself is based on a picture you've created in your mind, not the reality everyone else sees.

The disconnect between your image of yourself and reality can fracture your relationship with yourself. Did you ever fall in love with someone's appearance and then hate him when you heard him speak? Your perception of that person didn't match the reality. You can't carry on a relationship like that for very long. In the same way, your relationship with yourself cannot be healthy if you are dealing with a fantasy image made up in your mind.

I've learned that while it doesn't solve all problems or bring about world peace, mirror time can help build your relationship with yourself.

- Mirror time is not an excuse to keep everyone waiting for you to "put on your face." Actually, spending some time in front of the mirror can help you hone your makeup routine so you can be more efficient when you're on the go.

- One thing I discovered in the mirror one day was the small mole next to my nose. It wasn't always there, and I'm not sure when it developed. But I enjoy visiting the mole now when I look in the mirror because it is just like the one my grandmother had. It's a part of me that was part of her. Christine, I have had the dermatologist remove that mole three times! It keeps returning!

- When I traveled for work, I spent a lot of time projecting a public image for a client or my employer. It was difficult to uphold that image for several days in a row unless I had spent some mirror time at home, reconnecting with myself, trying on clothes, and organizing outfits for my next trip. Although I felt guilty at first, I learned the importance of that preparation time.

- I decided one day that I was never going to work up a sweat in a department store fitting room again. My mother always rushed me out and griped about my desire to fix my hair in front of the mirror. As an adult, I changed my shopping habit so that I can spend as much time in front of the fitting room mirror as I like. I always shop alone and at odd times, so my use of the fitting room is not inconveniencing anyone else.

There is value in standing around in front of the mirror (sorry, Mom). Although the concept might seem scary at first, facing your flaws in the florescent lighting of a department store fitting room, spending time in front of the mirror helps you develop a relationship with yourself built on reality. After all, everyone else looks at you all day, why should you be denied the privilege.

It's Not All About Looks

I don't know why I woke up at thirty-something with little or no self-esteem. It wasn't something my parents did or didn't do. There was no horrible bullying incident in my childhood or great failure to achieve some intended goal. It was probably the result of a unique set of circumstances that I will never be able to re-trace. But that's ok because I've decided the origin of this flaw doesn't matter.

You can't feel better about yourself while you are berating yourself for not being better. One thing I figured out is that a negative self-image creates a dangerous downward spiral.

Caught in the swirling momentum, your entire life can slide right by on its way to the basement — your parents' basement, that is, which is where you could end up at forty eating ice cream out of the container and watching reality TV in three-day-old yoga pants that your mother still calls sweat pants (she just won't let you have any glamour in your life).

My primary realizations about self-esteem include:

- Humans are meant to develop self-esteem during adolescence. How this is possible at the most awkward stage of your existence I don't know, but somewhere between surges in hormone levels and acne it should have sprouted along with breasts. Was everyone else's adolescence as dismal a failure as mine?

- Self-esteem is more difficult to develop later in life, but it's not your parents' fault, so leave them out of this. It's called SELF-esteem, so like other unexpected aspects of adult life, I have to figure this out for myself.

- Physical appearance and self-esteem have an unusual relationship. Even the most gorgeous people in the world don't necessarily have good self-esteem. I don't personally know any of these people, but I assume this to be true based on the fact that models, ballet dancers, and movie stars sometimes suffer from issues like anorexia.

- A lack of self-esteem can make you do destructive things like eat junk food and binge watch reality television, and it keeps you from taking the necessary risks to move your life forward like going outside or talking to real people.

- You need a healthy sense of self-esteem to live a happy, productive life. It may even be more essential criteria than intelligence or great hair.

It turns out that you have to drop the criticism if you're going to feel better about yourself. Sarcasm is my favorite form of humor, but I've learned my lesson about the toll it can take on self-esteem. It's only funny for a moment, and then it is real and sad and destructive.

How to Stop the Swirling

Did you ever notice that there is this critical little voice inside your head that sounds just like your mother, or your father, or your Grandma Elvira? I'm not sure at what point in my adult life I realized that the criticism conveniently came with me no matter where I went. I even moved to another state for a few years, but it was there, too.

The worst part was when I had the opportunity, and the strength, to confront my critics. I imagine that during my blaming years, my father developed an instinct to duck every time his phone rang. As my only surviving parent, he was naturally the one to catch all the criticism coming back at him.

My low moods always found their way to my father's ear. Dug into a poor-me position, I would finally trace some great flaw in my life back to something he said when I was six. Never one to really hold back, I'd call and confront him with his own quote thinking it would somehow resolve my current issue.

One day I was sure I knew the exact moment when he crushed my confidence for good, so I couldn't help calling to explain it to him. I reminded him of the day when I was six and heading to a birthday party for the kid down the street. Dad handed me a pen and told me to write my name on the card, but I made a mistake in forming one of the letters. Always the dramatic one, Dad said, "You can't even write your name without making a mistake?!"

This was it, the clincher. I had clearly illustrated how my father's characteristic criticism stomped out my young flame of confidence, making it not my fault. The only problem was that he didn't remember that day. He didn't remember saying that to me, and was sure he was only ever proud of my abilities. If he raised his voice to me at all it was only in frustration that we were running late and he had caught the dog sleeping on the couch again.

For all these years I carried this unintended critical message that I could never do anything right. His voice rang in my head every time I made a mistake, put a run in my stockings getting dressed too quickly, misspelled a word on the board in front of the class, or inadvertently insulted the boss' wife (to be fair, I didn't know she was the drunk blonde at the office Christmas party).

It turns out that Dad never even said that. Or he didn't't say it that way. Or he just meant it for the moment; after all, at six years old I should have been able to write my name flawlessly. I was the one who turned it into a mantra, carried it for thirty years, and applied it to any action I was not proud of. Instead of simply admitting I miss-spelled a word, I let it be a sign of some developmental flaw in my character by listening to the voice in my head.

Dad's voice was joined by my mother's voice telling me to hurry up any time I tried on clothes in a department store (I could never move fast enough for that woman) and Grandma Elvira's general "bad girl" assessment that was likely to pop up at anytime. For someone who spent a lot of time alone in my twenties and thirties, I certainly heard a lot of people telling me what I wasn't doing right.

Sometime after the umpteenth confrontation with the representative of the critical voices in my head, I decided there had to be a better way. Rehashing random moments of my childhood was not achieving the desired effect. I was spending hours wallowing in disappointment and depression not getting any relief. In fact, the confrontations were exacerbating the situation and eroding my relationship with my family.

I don't remember where I first heard the suggestion that I simply change the message. I don't dare to speculate since my recollection of the voices in my head is so unreliable. But someone, some book, some diligent therapist, some spirit from beyond told me I didn't have to listen to the voices in my head anymore.

One day I realized that although I wasn't ready to claim those voices, the head they were resonating in was my own, and I could kick them out. I didn't have to continue to live my life according to outdated, miss-interpreted, childhood messages. I could tell my brain what to think rather than allowing it to tell me how to feel.

Changing the Tune

When I was a little girl and I got into a funk, my mother would often suggest I change my tune. She would suggest a different activity or change the subject of conversation, but I was usually slow to recover from a bad mood. Sometimes I would continue to mope and snark long enough to get some form of punishment, usually ten minutes on my bed. Removing me from the situation ended the punishment I was doling out to everyone else in the room.

My mother was always good at celebrating my accomplishments, though. And by accomplishments I mean the little things. She wasn't waiting for the gold medals or the blue ribbons. With Mom, I always got a little praise for a job well done, even one that was overdue, like cleaning my room.

Mom was very practical and I know she would say it was just a matter of giving credit where credit was due. Subconsciously, I relied on her praise rather than developing my own sense of self-esteem. One day when she was sick and too weak to manage on her own, I helped her entertain some dear friends who wanted to come visit. I set up a tray for tea before I went out, so all Mom needed to do was boil the water.

When I came back after the visit, she thanked me for the help and noticed that I had set the tray with matching china cups instead of random selections from our mug collection. She told me she appreciated that I always had an eye for elegant details. I didn't even know she noticed that about me.

That simple compliment from my mother is one of the moments in my life that I've learned from. Not right away, of course. Life's lessons come slow to me. But over time I've learned to be that voice of praise for myself.

It was scary at first when I realized that my main source of positive feedback was gone. I didn't think I could survive. I wasn't sure I had learned enough from her to be my own cheerleader. My perspective was always critical, to focus on the failures with those voices in my head, but over time I was able to change my tune.

Here's what I figured out about how to deal with the voices inside my head:

- My family loves me and always wants what's best for me, but they don't always know what that is. Those messages became imbedded in my head when I was young and I interpreted them through a child's mind. They don't necessarily apply to situations in my grown-up life.

- Knowing when to listen to the voices is an important skill to develop. That voice that says look for traffic just before I step off the curb should not be ignored. I've outgrown the one that always holds me back from taking creative risks, though. That was meant for a vulnerable young child who Mom and Dad wanted to protect from the disappointment of failure.

- Always and never statements are seldom accurate. Those voices in my head that say I always make mistakes or never get it right are inflammatory. When I hear those voices, I can quickly refute them by thinking of just one instance where I didn't make a mistake and I did get it right. With their accuracy debunked, those voices have no credibility.

- It's important to exercise control over my adult brain. Part of being an adult is taking responsibility, and I'm in charge of me now. I don't have to pay attention to every idea that pops into my head. It's MY head! I get to decide what to think and how to evaluate my own actions.

The Importance of Language

Of course, language is important. Two English teachers raised me, and I use language to make a living. When I was growing up, inadequate antecedents and other usage issues were normal dinner table conversation. I have always believed that what you say is not quite as important as the eloquence with which you say it, and leaving out commas creates unacceptable ambiguity.

We never really talked about the connection between language and behavior, though. That one I had to figure out for myself. As a teacher I learned that writing is a reflection of the thought process. If a student's paragraph structure was poor, for example, his thoughts on the topic were probably not well formed, either. It is a natural extension, then, to see that language can color our perception of reality.

It's no wonder, then, that if the little voice inside your head is saying, "I'm so stupid," you get caught in a cycle of making mistakes over and over again. My sister grew up hearing that I was the pretty one and she was the smart one. She took this to mean that she was not pretty, (absolutely not true — her smile lights up the room) and internalized one of those erroneous messages. As she came to grips with her mistaken perception, she decided to share it with me. Of course, if I am the pretty one, I must not be smart, right? She continues to remind me how pretty I am every time I make a mistake.

The language that other people use when they describe us has an effect on our sense of self-esteem, especially if we adopt that language and use it on ourselves. So, language is a great tool for positive reinforcement. Unfortunately, many of us don't use it that way, and it adds to our downward spiral.

That's the thing about sarcasm...in order to be funny, there has to be a grain of truth to it. So while everyone is laughing at the zinger you just received for having your shirt on inside out, you are absorbing a negative message that will no doubt be repeated in your head many times.

Sarcasm is a veiled form of criticism delivered in a humorous way. Criticism is really at the heart of language that can erode the self-esteem. I always thought that a quick wit was a positive part of my character, and I could laugh at myself when I was the brunt of the joke (well, sometimes). Really my goal in life was to never be in that position, which many times meant striking first.

Like many epiphanies in my life, I first noticed the effects of critical comments on someone else. Listening to someone I love use sarcasm to lighten a tense situation by berating herself got my attention. I'm sure I had witnessed this routine before, but for some reason it struck me that day. As she was caught in a moment of extreme stress and self-doubt, I was impressed to see her laughing, not crying.

The criticism she lobbed at herself made me laugh and cringe at the same time. I wouldn't let anyone else say those things about her. I was actually offended and wanted to scream, "Stop. Shut Up. You can't say that." Knowing her as I do, I understood this was a reflex. Her natural reaction to failure was to blame herself. That's a reaction I could identify with. I do the same thing.

Changing my tune meant changing the language I use on myself. Here are some pointers:

- When I hear those voices in my head saying negative things about me, I stop them and quickly evaluate the message. If any part of it is incorrect, I ignore the whole thing. I choose to evaluate my behavior on a case-by-case basis, not use some generalized mantra.

- If I am at fault, I can accept responsibility without feeling like a complete failure. Making this one mistake does not negate my whole life. I am still a good person who just has some flaws.

- Pre-emptive messages can be the worst. No one needs a devil on her shoulder telling her she's a failure as she prepares to tackle the impossible situation of the day. I've learned to turn these messages to my advantage. "OMG, look what I'm doing. I can't do that," becomes, "OMG, look what I'm doing. I am fierce!"

- The power of positive thinking may seem silly, but by adopting a couple positive mantras for tough times, I've managed to become my own cheerleader. As I stroll into a high-pressure meeting with a confident smile on my face, I'm usually mumbling, "I can do this," under my breath.

- I can change my perspective by changing my language. When I'm in a scary situation and feeling uncomfortable, my mantra becomes, "I'm ok." It helps me to assess the situation objectively and recognize that my anxiety is unfounded. With several repetitions of the phrase, it actually becomes true.

It's surprising to realize the empowerment you can get from taking control of your own thoughts. I've come to understand that my self-esteem is a relationship between me and myself. Other people's opinions of me are not part of it.

As I turn forty, I understand that I can create the messages in my head that affect my sense of self-worth. I am responsible for my own wellbeing, so why wouldn't I talk to myself in a kind and supportive tone. Why can't I be my own cheerleader? I used to think it was because I know myself too well. I know all of my flaws and couldn't lie to myself. Now I realize that I know myself better than that. I see past the flaws, and when I focus on my successes, they build on one another.

CHAPTER FIVE

"When I feel like there are not enough hours in the day, I spend some time staring at the ceiling. Inactivity completely resets my clock."

Seeking Happiness

Scan the self-help shelves in any bookstore and you realize what everyone wants. Ok, they want to be thin, but after that they want to be happy. We are all searching for happiness. My question is, if that is your ultimate goal, what will you do when you reach it? That's the problem with goals, you either have to have an endless supply of them or you have to set goals you can never attain. Otherwise, your life may come to an abrupt halt one day. Happiness seems to be one of those goals that people won't let themselves reach. Maybe because they don't know what they would do next.

I have spent forty years searching for happiness right along with the rest of America. When I was a kid, I knew I'd be happy when I became an adult. After all, adults got to do all the fun stuff. They could stay up late at night and watch television. Adults got to decide when to have friends over, when to eat dinner out, when it was time to play; they had all the power.

I could see how happy my life would be when I was an adult. Plus, my parents always dangled adulthood out there like a carrot. They would tell me that when I was older I'd be able to make certain decisions for myself – like when to wear a jacket, what time to go to bed, how far to ride my bike. This was supposed to be of some comfort while they reminded me of the here and now and that I was being grounded for disobeying some decision they had made for me. I was quite sure my parents had never really been children themselves.

In adolescence I thought I was closer to adulthood, but somehow there were more things I could not do and decide for myself. Once again I was expected to take solace in knowing that "someday" I'd be making these decisions for myself. But for right now, the tube top was an inappropriate choice and I must change my clothes if I expected to leave the house. Also, jeans, or dungarees as my mother called them, were not acceptable attire for school. Never mind that the good ones cost more than my school shoes.

Then, I went off to college, which undoubtedly would be fun. College was like one giant sleepover party in the movies. Surely, happiness would be found in a dorm room or a lecture hall or even the student center. There would be gobs of happiness at all-night study sessions and beer parties. Never mind that I didn't drink beer; I could learn. Life-long friendships would be made at college, which would insure life-long happiness.

I packed my tube tops and dungarees and boxed up all my shoes. Hey, if I was going to finally be happy, I wanted to be sure I had on the right outfit. Somehow I got the notion that a footlocker was required for college, so I scoured the city for a used steamer trunk.

My grandfather, the only one who was willing to brave my driving practice, agreed to accompany me on a trip to the "used furniture store" section of downtown. Grandpa Bill wasn't afraid of anything. The deal was, I got to drive; he was just the fully licensed adult in the car. We both knew Grandpa was the muscle on this trip. His presence kept the idle stoup-sitters from approaching this almost grown up on the sidewalk outside the stores. Once inside, Grandpa negotiated a price on the trunk that even a soon-to-be poor college student could afford.

That day was a glimpse of the elusive happiness I was about to gain, until we got back home with the prized trunk. Grandpa made it clear he would not be a passenger in my vehicle again. And my aunt strongly expressed her disapproval for my taking her father into "those" neighborhoods. The implication was that I was not ready to be an adult because I demonstrated poor decision-making skills. Forget the fact that nothing bad happened; it's what could have happened.

Cleaning and re-papering the inside of that trunk became a labor of love. Having your own footlocker was like a rite of passage. Every college graduate I knew had one. This would be mine to take with me into that happy place –- adulthood.

As it turns out, there wasn't much happiness at college, at least not for me. The dorm rooms were much smaller than any I had seen in the movies. In fact, mine was smaller than my bedroom at home, and I was expected to share it with a complete stranger. Hey, I had given up sharing a bedroom with my sister when I was about twelve. How was this supposed to work?

My first roommate was a senior who was not expecting to share "her" room. She seemed friendly enough when she invited me to the bars with her and her other friends. But I was very young for college and not familiar with the party scene. Too shy to venture out, I spent the first several nights alone in my room. One day for fun, I walked into town and got myself some ice cream. Then, I called home on a pay phone and cried to my little sister about how lonely it was at college.

I went through three roommates the first semester – the senior who went to the bars every night of the week, the girl from Brooklyn who couldn't be my friend because I was the only white girl on the hall, and the Jersey girl who already had enough friends. College was the opposite of happiness for me. But I knew if I could just finish college and get out into the real world, then I'd be happy.

In the real world I could have my own apartment and work full time. This arrangement would afford me more privacy and the capital to support my Ben & Jerry's habit. Unlike the time I spent all my money on a great dress and then had to eat in the cafeteria for the rest of the month, I would be able to buy what I wanted. I knew what happiness looked like. It was me with an apartment in Manhattan, stylish suits and dresses for work, and a classy boyfriend. All of this would come to me as soon as I finished college.

Funny thing about happiness – it doesn't seem to just knock on your door. One day I woke up and I was living and working in Manhattan. I didn't feel any more glamorous than I did in college, however, and I wasn't really any happier. I went through two roommates in six months, but I couldn't afford to live alone. I was so bored at work that I often had to fight to keep my eyes open in the late afternoon. My classy boyfriend wasn't classy at all. He was just a leftover from college that I clung to for security.

I did have some great clothes, though. My boss and I wore the same size; she was always bringing me hand-me-downs. I developed a great collection of silk tops, designer suits, and even summer casual sets. She dressed me for a family picnic on Long Island that summer. I was as cool and sophisticated as that family has ever seen. When I came back to work on Monday, my boss told me not to return her outfit; it was mine.

I spent the next ten to fifteen years of my life chasing happiness, believing it was just around the next corner. I moved home, changed careers, changed jobs, and changed boyfriends. I got married; I got unmarried. I worked full-time; I worked part-time; I didn't work at all. I went back to relationships that hadn't worked out thinking I was happier then. I was lonely and sometimes miserable, but sure I'd be happy once I had the right job, the right house, the right boyfriend.

Found It!

One day, in the midst of all the chaos of my highly imperfect life, I sat down and found happiness. People had always told me you have to be happy with yourself. I thought what that meant was that you had to make yourself perfect so you could be happy. Why would anyone be happy with an imperfect self? I wouldn't because I know I can do better.

I spent years analyzing my performance on every task – from baking a cake to entertaining friends – to figure out how I could do it better next time. I knew that one day I could be flawless. If I were funnier, I would have more friends. If I worked harder, I would have a better job. If I were smarter, I would have more money. There was just no end to the improvements I could make, but I wasn't giving up my quest for happiness. I knew I deserved to find happiness.

By my mid-thirties I was heading for a breakdown. Time was passing me by. Other people my age, my peers we can assume, were living happy and productive lives while I seemed to just be getting started. At this rate, I would run out of time before settling into my happy life with the right job, the right house, and the right man. At one point, I worked three jobs, seven days a week, until I reached near collapse. Then I got a better job, so I could quit the other two. Soon that wasn't good enough and I started pushing for a promotion, a raise, and an office.

I began to realize that my life had become a vicious cycle in which I no sooner achieved a small gain when I was pushing hard for the next level. The obvious question suddenly occurred to me: what am I doing this for? For the first time I began to doubt if I would ever reach happiness. At thirty-something, I no longer had my whole life ahead of me. Time constraints required that I give up some options and choose a path.

It was sad to face the fact that I would never be a child prodigy or a teenage star. Time had stolen those options from me. It was also probably too late to become an astronaut or an Olympic athlete. Luckily, I never really had an interest in either of those fields. But it was time to face the reality that I could no longer be anything I wanted. My options were now limited.

But where had I gone wrong? How did I squander my youth? I had been hyper-focused on achievement since college but hadn't achieved anything. I wasn't the best, biggest, greatest, and most important anything. I didn't live in a castle or earn boat-loads of money. I wasn't married to a prince and hadn't given birth to baby Einsteins. Happiness had completely eluded my grasp.

I found happiness when I gave up reaching for it and realized I had it all along. It sounds trite but it's true. Did you ever notice that an hour spent staring at the ceiling is longer than an hour spent multi-tasking? When I feel like there are not enough hours in the day, I spend some time staring at the ceiling. Inactivity completely resets my clock. Finding happiness was simply a matter of pressing reset, too.

We each define happiness for ourselves, and we also decide when and how to experience it. Again, it sounds too good to be true but it is. Once I realized that I had allowed the world around me to define happiness for me, it was easy to get happy. I simply re-defined it for myself. So now happiness is working too many hours for too little pay and no respect. Just kidding — that's reality.

Happiness is this feeling I get inside when I see the beautiful colors of the sunset on my commute home at the end of the day. It reminds me that I am a very small part of a wondrous universe where all things are possible, but I don't personally have to achieve them. And we all look at the same setting sun, whether from an old pick-up truck or a shiny new convertible.

It seems impossible to find happiness in a simple sunset when you've spent your whole life looking for it around every corner and turning yourself inside out to achieve it. If I hadn't come to this realization myself, I wouldn't believe it. If someone told me, and they probably did at some point, that happiness was in the small wonders of life, I would have smiled and walked away. That may be true for children and the non-thinking, but I am an intelligent, highly sophisticated adult who does not enjoy keeping company with vacuous people.

But I never noticed the happiness in a sunset because I was busy striving and achieving. The more I did, the bigger that elusive happiness became. I wasn't looking for it in the small things; I was expecting to be hit on the head with it, engulfed with a happiness so pervasive I could see nothing else. My mother always warned me about missing the boat – well I missed that one big time. The non-thinkers were right; who knew?

What it's Really Made of

In my twenties, I spent a lot of time driving. I always loved to drive. I loved the feeling of acceleration that pushed me back into the seat, the freedom of "just going". The display of motor skills typically reserved for the male population gave me a particular thrill. I observed the male drivers in my life, really listened to their trash-talk about fast driving, and practiced when I was alone in my car. To me, there was nothing like the feeling of dropping it into fourth gear and gliding through the S-turns at a constant rate of speed. There was one certain place where the highway passed through the city with a series of interchanges, typical of most interstates in medium-sized cities. I would leave my cruise control set to highway speed and see how far into the city highway maze I could go before losing my nerve and slowing down.

Of course, those moments of thrill seeking did not add up to true happiness in my mind. I knew I would be happy someday when I had a car that could keep up with me. I deserved a vehicle that would allow me to reach the sort of speed I was capable of handling. (When I reached thirty-something and got my motorcycle license, I thought back to the thrill-seeking driving habits of my twenties and realized the Universe was organized in such a way for a reason.)

I used to drive long trips by myself. I once drove from North Carolina to Key West non-stop. Driving highways at night made me feel like I was beating the traffic (a small sign of success), so I sped along under cover of darkness. During the two years I lived in North Carolina, I drove the ten hours back to New York alone frequently. I wasn't going to let distance or convention keep me from the adventures I created for myself. Looking back I realize I was just running away, always seeking happiness in the last place I had seen it.

Those long drives gave me time to be myself. With the music blaring, I was flying down the highway singing at the top of my voice. I was sure I'd be happy when my musical talent was discovered; unfortunately, I have yet to roll up next to any music executives at a stoplight. The music let me release my emotions in the privacy of my car. I'd be singing away and then all of a sudden the tears would come. I'd listen very carefully to the lyrics to see what my subconscious was reacting to. I believed there was a message in there for me, giving me important insight to the meaning of my life and what I should do to fix it.

What I know now is that songs are written to sell records, not instruct to the listener in life's lessons. They're not really talking about me or events that could take place in my life. If there is any similarity between the lyrics and my life, it is a coincidence (and I had better make some changes so my life reads less like a soap-opera).

Even without the music, my mind wandered onto all sorts of topics on those long drives. Sometimes I would find myself reliving some embarrassing moment or creating what-if scenarios like what would I do if my parents were killed in a plane crash or what if the car next to me suddenly veers into my lane and I am forced through a series of impossible maneuvers in order to spare the life of the driver in the on-coming lane. There were some very emotional times spent in my car on long road trips.

As I approach my fortieth birthday, I am happy to report I have gotten over all of that unnecessary emotional baggage. Not that I don't worry that bad things could happen to people I love. But I've come to realize that my thoughts are my own. I control them, not the other way around. As my time on this planet gets shorter (let's face it, forty could be the beginning of the end), it becomes more important to me to spend as much of it as possible in a blissful state.

I no longer waste time and emotion on mental exercises. If I'm in the middle of an actual crisis I react to the best of my ability. After all, I've spent nearly forty years preparing myself for the worst and coming up with contingency plans. One of my mother's deathbed wisdoms was that everyone is doing the best they can at any given moment. We can count on that and it is all we can expect. I trust that the next time I am in a crisis situation, therefore, I will do my best even though I haven't had time to plan and practice. The rest of my time can be spent in productive or relaxing pursuits, not preparing for disaster or reliving old nightmares.

Happiness happens whenever I let it. By blocking out bad thoughts, I allow happy ones a chance to take over. Who wouldn't rather be happy if given the choice? More and more, I am conscious of the fact that I have that choice, and I choose to be happy. I can shut down those negative thoughts and look for a sunrise. If I can't find a sunrise, I can remember the last one I saw. It puts a smile on my face every time.

A Special Section on Smiling

Smiling is another one of those happiness related topics that I've learned a lot about in the last forty years. Forcing yourself to smile can actually improve your mood. Take this test: the next time you feel down, smile for no reason at all. It will feel strange at first; you may want to practice when you're alone. When one of your co-workers dumps their project on you at the last minute, smile and say ok. Smile as the boss instructs you in a task you'd rather claw your eyes out than undertake.

Your mood will improve if only because you are laughing at yourself. In certain situations, you can derive some pleasure from knowing that people are wondering what you're hiding behind that smile. Others will think you've lost your mind, but the shock value will be good for a little laugh. Eventually, you'll realize that other people, even the unpleasant ones, cannot make you unhappy. Happiness can persist in the face of adversity, or more importantly, ambivalence.

On the days when I'm depressed because there is nothing to be happy about – no major life events, no unexpected incidence of good fortune – I realize I can be happy anyway. Just pasting a smile on my face seems to remind my brain that happiness should be the default state, not the exception. If my hair is not on fire, I'm probably happy and just don't realize it. The smile reminds me.

Since I'm sure all babies smile, there must be some point at which I lost it. Maybe around adolescence I started considering myself to be a serious person. The reason I didn't smile a lot was that I was intelligent and responsible, wise beyond my years, and all that thinking took energy. Smiling was a sign of bliss, that empty-headed sort of happiness reserved for cute, curly-haired blondes.

For the first ten years of my life I tried to be cute and sweet without much success. I was just too big, smart and brunette to hide it. I was always the tallest girl in my class, even taller than all the boys some years. And I could not get over my compulsion to shout out the right answers and follow the teacher's directions. I tried to giggle, speak softly, and wear little pink outfits with lace and ruffles, but I never got the kind of attention and coddling shown to the petite air-headed girls in class.

So I accepted the fact that I was not cute and moved on with my serious self. I turned my attention to being smart, responsible and grown-up and my youthful smile faded. I never developed a nervous giggle. When I was shy or embarrassed I just kept still and got quiet. In strange situations I would listen intently until I could think of an intelligent comment to contribute. My face adopted a permanent serious expression as I moved into adulthood.

Then there were the "smile" people. You know, those people who come at you out of nowhere and insist, "Smile!" They act as if they have all the answers when I'm sure they know nothing. If they had a clue they would not suggest that the expression on my face was at all relevant to the conversation. Even worse are the "smile for me" people. What on earth gives them the right to make demands? I don't owe them anything.

I don't know what happened to my seriousness campaign. It probably wore me out. After nearly forty years of making the world safe for intelligent, non-smiling people, I guess I decided it wasn't worth the effort. Very often, it did not have the desired effect.

Actually, I first tried the smile thing as an expression of my personal sarcasm. I had finally learned to keep those comments to myself; in many situations it is safer that way. So the smile came about as I was almost unable to hold back a zinger. The sarcastic smile felt good. Eventually, it lost its edge and became comforting in its own right. Now I just smile for the shear enjoyment of it (exercising the facial muscles will combat a sagging jaw line as I enter my forties, too).

Happiness is a Choice

Acting happy, of course, isn't the answer. If it were, I would have given up when I got this far. Come on, who wants to believe that happiness is just an act. I'm good but I could never fool myself with an act for the rest of my life. Acting happy was just the quickest and easiest way to counteract years of self-imposed unhappiness. Plus, I'm all about control. Believing that I can control my happiness, I can choose to be happy even when people and circumstances around me seem to discourage my happiness; that was huge for me. If I'm in control of my happiness, then it's a breeze. I know I can do it.

I choose to be happy right now, as I approach my fortieth birthday, with just the money, the house and the man I have in my life at this moment. I am tired of rushing around to be better, to be more, to measure up to some arbitrary scale. There are things I can't go back and undo. For instance, if happiness requires an Ivy League degree, I'm screwed. I graduated from a state school, and there are no do-overs.

So, I begin with the sunrise. I have the good fortune of commuting east every morning and west in the evening. When I stopped complaining about the sun always being in my eyes, I found happiness in commuter traffic. I see the sunrise every morning as a symbol of a new beginning. Whatever I screwed up at work the day before is history. The sunrise marks the beginning of a new day, a new opportunity to get it right this time. If the sunrise were a symbol of a new boss, this might really be true. But for twenty minutes alone in my car in the morning, I make the rules.

And so goes my new definition of happiness:

- Happiness is knowing I have enough. I never knew how much was enough and was sure there was no such thing as too much. But I choose to be happy right now with what I have, so therefore it must be enough. In fact, I'm quite sure that at any given moment of my life I have had enough. (Sometimes I say it right out loud, "I've had enough!")

- Happiness is knowing there are people in this world who love me and are flawed just like me – or in other more disturbing ways. When I stopped criticizing their tactics and questioning their motives, I found people who love me unconditionally. They are the same people I thought were not capable because of their own dysfunctions. Now I realize they don't love me less when they go into rehab and can't call me for thirty days. They love me more by trying to get themselves straightened out.

- Happiness in knowing I can stand still and the earth continues to rotate. The sun comes up every morning and sets at the end of the day. I can partake in these events, just like everyone else, no matter where I am, no matter who I am, no matter what I've accomplished — just stand still and look up. Knowing that gives me hope, so no matter what happens to me, I can always experience happiness.

- Happiness is a state of being I enter anytime I want to, by reminding myself I am a human-being, not a human-doing. All the striving and achieving mean nothing in this area. My existence on this planet, as unique as a snowflake, is the value I bring.

Redefining happiness allowed me to slow down and stop striving for a while. Since the re-defined happiness was already in my grasp, I could catch my breath. Once I stopped moving so fast, I looked at everything in my life a little differently...and happiness flourished.

Of course, now that I realize I had happiness all along, I only wish I had figured this out sooner. But, I resolve not to bring regrets with me into my forties, so this one dies here. And all that stuff at the beginning of the chapter about goals goes out the window, too. Happiness is not a goal; it is a starting point. My life is not complete because I have found happiness. Because what I found with it is an understanding of what happiness really is.

This state of mind we call happiness is an essential part of life. Everyone has access to it at any time. From a place of happiness we can achieve great things. The struggle is in trying to achieve anything without a basic sense of happiness. Without happiness there is angst, which is a huge hindrance to accomplishment. It is like trying to swim to shore with a wet blanket on your back; it is the cliché "ball and chain" around your ankle.

AFTERWORD

While I finished writing this book and going through the publishing process, my life continued to evolve. Although I chose my fortieth birthday as a milestone at which to stop and take stock of the journey thus far, learning and growing did not stop there.

The most surprising development is how my relationship with my father has evolved. Maybe this is how it goes for all forty-somethings. I don't know. I felt like I did so much growing in this area during my thirties that it was probably as good as it was going to get. Part of that made me feel accomplished to have advanced this far, and in part it made me feel sad, as if I were accepting less than perfect to end the turmoil.

As it turns out, getting over the blaming years and forgiving my father for my childhood was just a milestone in this relationship journey. To be honest, I'd have to sprinkle in a little forgiving myself as part of achieving that milestone. From the time I finished writing the initial draft of this book to now, we've evolved a little more.

My father, the man I thought had turned me into a low-achieving n'er-do-well with his sarcastic and unrelenting criticism, became my trusted editor on this book project. I explained the project to him one day out of the blue and sent him a sample chapter to read. I knew it was well-written and that he would have to compliment me on the writing style, even if he didn't like the content.

Dad's initial reply was complimentary, but not enthusiastic about the overall project. It took some explaining for him to understand where I was going with this. Meanwhile, Dad had become the biggest supporter of my new writing career (to be fair, he didn't have much competition for that role) and he was editing all of my shorter pieces.

I knew my father was a writer and an educator, but it wasn't until he started working with me on my own writing that I saw his real strength. Dad is an excellent editor, for both content and mechanics. He finds those places where a thought is dropped and never resolved, or where the theme needs to be repeated to reinforce the strength of the piece. He appreciates a good metaphor, and he hasn't forgotten any of that old-school grammar he started his career peddling to nine-year-olds.

I spent years complaining that my father didn't know what I was capable of. He seemed to ignore the details of my professional life, dropping in on occasion to say, "You can do that?" All that time, it never occurred to me that I didn't really know what his intellectual capacity was either. I knew he was smart about "book stuff," but I didn't know his true strengths.

Dad became my editor and cheerleader on this book project. I can still remember the day I emailed him the complete manuscript to review for the first time. After I pressed "send", I held my breath. Each hour that passed without a reply from him drove me closer to realizing I had just bared my soul to someone who never wanted to know me that well.

The most surprising part of our alliance is that I welcomed his criticism and ended up trusting him with every question I had about what to include, how to say it, and how it might be perceived. His guidance on this project was both professional and compassionate. Having my father on the inside of this project with me, dealing with some emotional content that we both shared, was comforting.

Although it was never my intension, I think this book served as the articulation of my apology to my father for the blaming years. Maybe it gave him the insight he was missing as to how I processed the events of my life and came up with the positions I did. Maybe he wasn't looking for that clarification, but he handled it well.

Whether this book sells one million copies or sits on a shelf collecting dust until the cover fades, I know my father is proud of my work. And, I am proud of the knowledge and guidance he had to offer. Of course, we still do not share the same political views and continue to avoid any substantive discussions on the matter, but that will have to be the next book.

ABOUT THE AUTHOR

Christine R. Andola is a freelance writer and native of Central New York whose work has been published in several regional and online magazines. She writes about food, health, business, and other topics. Christine has lived in the Southern Tier, the Hudson Valley, the North Country, and New York City, and has traveled a good portion of the Erie Canal. Who Knew? is her first book.

Printed in the United States
By Bookmasters